John Ford's The Fancies, Chaste and Noble: A Retelling

David Bruce

Published by David Bruce, 2022.

This is a work of fiction. Similarities to real people, places, or events are entirely coincidental.

JOHN FORD'S THE FANCIES, CHASTE AND NOBLE: A RETELLING

First edition. July 9, 2022.

ISBN: 979-8201064327

Written by David Bruce.

Table of Contents

Dedication

Dedicated to Carl Eugene Bruce and Josephine Saturday Bruce

My father, Carl Eugene Bruce, died on 24 October 2013. He used to work for Ohio Power, and at one time, his job was to shut off the electricity of people who had not paid their bills. He sometimes would find a home with an impoverished mother and some children. Instead of shutting off their electricity, he would tell the mother that she needed to pay her bill or soon her electricity would be shut off. He would write on a form that no one was home when he stopped by because if no one was home he did not have to shut off their electricity.

The best good deed that anyone ever did for my father occurred after a storm that knocked down many power lines. He and other linemen worked long hours and got wet and cold. Their feet were freezing because water got into their boots and soaked their socks. Fortunately, a kind woman gave my father and the other linemen dry socks to wear.

My mother, Josephine Saturday Bruce, died on 14 June 2003. She used to work at a store that sold clothing. One day, an impoverished mother with a baby clothed in rags walked into the store and started shoplifting in an interesting way: The mother took the rags off her baby and dressed the infant in new clothing. My mother knew that this mother could not afford to buy the clothing, but she helped the mother dress her baby and then she watched as the mother walked out of the store without paying.

***

The doing of good deeds is important. As a free person, you can choose to live your life as a good person or as a bad person. To be a good person, do good deeds. To be a bad person, do bad deeds. If you do good deeds, you will become good. If you do bad deeds, you will become bad. To become the person you want to be, act as if you already are that kind of person. Each of us chooses what kind of person we will become. To become a good person, do the things a good person does. To become a bad person, do the things a bad person does. The opportunity to take action to become the kind of person you want to be is yours.

Human beings have free will. According to the Babylonian Niddah 16b, whenever a baby is to be conceived, the Lailah (angel in charge of contraception) takes the drop of semen that will result in the conception and asks God, "Sovereign of the Universe, what is going to be the fate of this drop? Will it develop into a robust or into a weak person? An intelligent or a stupid person? A wealthy or a poor person?" The Lailah asks all these questions, but it does not ask, "Will it develop into a righteous or a wicked person?" The answer to that question lies in the decisions to be freely made by the human being that is the result of the conception.

A Buddhist monk visiting a class wrote this on the chalkboard: "EVERYONE WANTS TO SAVE THE WORLD, BUT NO ONE WANTS TO HELP MOM DO THE DISHES." The students laughed, but the monk then said, "Statistically, it's highly unlikely that any of you will ever have the opportunity to run into a burning orphanage and rescue an infant. But, in the smallest gesture of kindness — a warm smile, holding the door for the person behind you, shoveling the driveway of the elderly person next door — you have committed an act of immeasurable profundity, because to each of us, our life is our universe."

Cover Photo for John Ford's *The Fancies, Chaste and Noble*: A Retelling

Adina Voicu

https://pixabay.com/photos/girls-buddy-three-dresses-beauty-1487823/

Educate Yourself

Read Like A Wolf Eats

Be Excellent to Each Other

Books Then, Books Now, Books Forever

In this retelling, as in all my retellings, I have tried to make the work of literature accessible to modern readers who may lack some of the knowledge about mythology, religion, and history that the literary work's contemporary audience had.

Do you know a language other than English? If you do, I give you permission to translate this book, copyright your translation, publish or self-publish it, and keep all the royalties for yourself. (Do give me credit, of course, for the original retelling.)

I would like to see my retellings of classic literature used in schools, so I give permission to the country of Finland (and all other countries) to give copies of any or all of my retellings to all students forever. I also give permission to the state of Texas (and all other states) to give copies of this book to all students forever. I also give permission to all teachers to give copies of this book to all students forever.

Teachers need not actually teach my retellings. Teachers are welcome to give students copies of my eBooks as background material. For example, if they are teaching Homer's *Iliad* and *Odyssey*, teachers are welcome to give students copies of my *Virgil's* Aeneid: *A Retelling in Prose* and tell students, "Here's another ancient epic you may want to read in your spare time."

CAST OF CHARACTERS

Male Characters

OCTAVIO, Marquis of Siena.

TROYLO-SAVELLI, his nephew.

LIVIO, brother to Castamela.

ROMANELLO, brother to Flavia.

JULIO DE VARANA, lord of Camerino.

CAMILLO, attendant on Julio.

VESPUCCI, attendant on Julio.

FABRICIO, a merchant, Flavia's first husband.

NITIDO, a page, attendant on the Marquis.

SECCO, a barber, attendant on the Marquis.

SPADONE, attendant on the Marquis. Spadone is reputed to be a eunuch.

Female Characters

CASTAMELA, sister to Livio.

CLARELLA, one of the Fancies.

SILVIA, one of the Fancies.

FLORIA, one of the Fancies.

FLAVIA, wife to Julio.

MOROSA, an older woman who is guardian to the Fancies.

Scene

Siena, Italy.

Intertwined Plots:

Ford's play has many plots involving these characters:

• The bachelor Octavio, Marquis of Siena, has a "Bower of Fancies" for three young women whom he calls the "fancies" — Clarella, Silvia, and Floria. They are believed by some to be Octavio's harem — his sex partners.

• Livio and Castamela arrive at the court. His sister, Castamela, becomes a companion to the "fancies." Octavio and his nephew, Troylo-Savelli, pursue or seem to pursue her sexually or romantically.

• The spendthrift Fabricio has divorced his wife, Flavia, so she can marry Julio, a wealthy nobleman who has agreed to pay off Frabricio's debts. Two noblemen, Camillo and Vespucci, pursue Flavia sexually.

• The barber Secco marries Morosa, an older woman who serves as guardian of the Fancies. Secco, Morosa, Octavio's page Nitido, and Octavio's attendant Spadone engage in bawdy humor.

One theme of the play is that what we think we know about another person may not be true.

This play is a comedy: It has a happy ending.

Notes:

In this culture, a man of higher rank would use words such as "thee," "thy," "thine," and "thou" to refer to a servant. However, two close friends or a husband and wife could properly use "thee," "thy," "thine," and "thou" to refer to each other.

The word "sirrah" is a term usually used to address a man of lower social rank than the speaker. This was socially acceptable, but sometimes the speaker would use the word as an insult when speaking to a man whom he did not usually call "sirrah." Close friends, whether male or female, could also call each other "sirrah."

In this culture, wives call their husbands "lord."

PROLOGUE

An actor comes on stage and gives the Prologue:

"*The Fancies*! That's our play! In it is shown

"Nothing but what our author knows his own

"Without a learned theft."

In other words: This play is original with John Ford and is not plagiarized.

The actor continues:

"No servant here

"To some fair mistress borrows for his ear

"His lock [lovelock], his belt, his sword, the fancied grace

"Of any pretty ribbon ..."

Note: The "lock" is a lovelock, a long lock of hair tied in a ribbon and dangling from the left ear down to the shoulder. The actor states that John Ford is not like a lover (servant) borrowing items to dress up his play. John Ford's brain is good enough to write original plays.

The actor continues:

"... or, in place

"Of charitable friendship, is brought in

"A thriving gamester, that doth [who does] chance to win

"A lusty sum, while the good hand doth [does] ply him,

"And Fancies this or that to him sits by him."

In other words: John Ford is not like someone who sucks up to a winning gambler, presumably to get money. John Ford has enough of an independent income to write plays.

The actor continues:

"His [John Ford's] free invention runs but in conceit

"Of mere imaginations; there's the height

"Of what he writes ..."

In other words: This is John Ford's own play, written with his own ideas and imagination and written as well as he can write it.

The actor continues:

"... which if traduced by some,

"'Tis well, he says, he's far enough from home."

In other words: Perhaps some critics will traduce this play, but John Ford will be away during opening night.

The actor continues:

"For you, for him, for us, then this remains,

"Fancy your own opinions for our pains."

In other words: You, the audience, will make up your own minds about the worth of this play.

CHAPTER 1
— 1.1 —

Troylo-Savelli and Livio spoke together in an apartment in the palace in Siena, Italy. Troylo-Savelli was the nephew of Octavio, Marquis of Siena. Livio was the brother of Castamela.

Troylo-Savelli was criticizing Livio, who had reputation but little money.

"Do, do," he said, sarcastically. "Be deliberately desperate: It is manly. Build on your reputation! Such a fortune of reputation may furnish your tables with food, trim your servants' liveries, enrich your heirs with purchase of a patrimony — an estate — that shall hold out beyond the waste of riotous living, stick honors on your heraldry, with titles as swelling and as numerous as may likely grow to a pretty volume, here's eternity!

"All this reputation, by the Virgin Mary, can do. Indeed, what can reputation not do?"

Livio replied, "Such language from a gentleman so noble in his quality as you are, deserves, in my weak judgment, pity rather than contempt."

Troylo-Savelli said, "Could thou consider, Livio, the fashion of the times, their study, practice — nay, their ambitions — thou would soon distinguish between the abject lowness of a poverty and the applauded triumph of abundance, although the abundance is accomplished by the meanest service."

Livio had a good reputation, but he could fare better by paying more attention to the gaining of a higher social position and a greater amount of wealth.

Troylo-Savelli continued, "Wherein shall you betray your guilt to common censure, waiving the private burden of your reputation, by rising up to greatness, or at least to plenty, which now buys greatness?"

Livio could do something that would bring him wealth and greatness, but doing that thing would cause him to be widely condemned.

Livio said, "Troylo-Savelli plays merrily on my needs."

He thought that Troylo-Savelli was mocking him.

Speaking in the third person, Troylo-Savelli said, "Troylo-Savelli speaks to the friend he loves, to his own Livio.

"Look, I beg of you, go through the Great Duke's court in Florence, number his favorites, and then examine by what steps some chief officers in state have reached the height they stand in."

Livio replied, "They have reached the height they stand in by their merits."

Troylo-Savelli replied sarcastically, "Right, by their merits."

He then mentioned some ways they had reached the height they stand in:

"Well he merited the intendments — the office of supervision — over the galleys at the city of Ligorne, not far from here and from Florence. He was made the grand collector of the customs there. Who am I speaking of? He who led the prince to his wife's chaste bed, and stood nearby in his nightgown, fearing the jest might be discovered. Wasn't it handsome? The lady does not yet know about it."

To order to achieve wealth and social standing, the man had let the prince pretend to be him and have sex with his wife.

Livio said, "That is most impossible."

Troylo-Savelli gave another sarcastic example of merit:

"He merited well to wear a robe of fine camlet who trained his brother's daughter, scarcely a girl, to go into the arms of Mont-Argentorato, while the young lord of Telamon, her husband, was sent by boat to France to study how to act and speak at court, under, truly, a pretext of employment. Employment! Yes, of honor!"

Livio said, "You're well read in mysteries of state."

Troylo-Savelli said, "Here in Siena, bold Julio de Varana, lord of Camerine, held it no blemish to his blood and greatness from a plain merchant to buy with a thousand ducats his wife; indeed, he held it no blemish to justify the purchase. He procured it by a dispensation from Rome, allowed and warranted."

The dispensation released the wife from her marriage vows to the merchant. Enough money can procure such a dispensation, even in a Catholic country.

Troylo-Savelli continued, "It was thought by his physicians that she was a creature that agreed best with the cure of the disease his present new infirmity then labored in."

The disease perhaps was melancholy, but if sin can be regarded as an illness, the disease may have been lechery.

Troylo-Savelli continued, "Yet these are things that in the sight of the world are advanced, employed, and eminent."

Livio said, "At best it is but a goodly panderism."

The world was putting a good face on the selling of women.

Troylo-Savelli said, "It's a shrewd business! Thou child in thrift, thou fool of honesty, is it a disparagement for gentlemen, for friends of lower rank, to do the offices of necessary kindness without fee for one another, courtesies of course, mirths of society; when petty mushrooms, transplanted from their dunghills, spread on mountains, and pass for cedars by their servile flatteries on great men's vices?"

Mushrooms are social upstarts: men who grow quickly in wealth and social status the way a mushroom grows overnight. One way to become such a mushroom, Troylo-Savelli was saying, was to engage in this kind of panderism.

Troylo-Savelli continued, "'Pander'! Thou are deceived. The word includes preferment — promotions and advancement! It is a title of dignity. I could add somewhat more else."

Livio said, "Add anything of reason."

Troylo-Savelli said, "Castamela, thy beauteous sister, like a precious tissue — a rich fabric — not shaped into a garment fit for wearing, lacks the adornments of the workman's cunning skill to set the richness of the piece at view, although she in herself is all wonder.

"Come, I'll tell thee. There may be a way — know that I love thee, Livio — to fix this jewel in a ring of gold, yet lodge it in a cabinet of ivory — white, pure, unspotted ivory.

"Suppose that Livio himself shall keep the key to it?"

Livio replied, "Oh, sir, create me what you please of yours; do this, you are another nature."

If his sister, Castamela, were to marry the right person, then she could have a wealthy husband and Livio could advance in society.

Livio was willing for this to happen, and if Troylo-Savelli could make it happen, Livio would be beholden to him. He would be Troylo-Savelli's creature — he would owe his wealth and social position to him.

To Livio, this seemed like a socially acceptable form of panderism.

Troylo-Savelli said, "Be, then, pliable to my first rules of your advancement."

The entrance of Octavio and Nitido, who was Octavio's page — personal attendant — interrupted him.

Troylo-Savelli said, "Look! Octavio, my good uncle, the great Marquis of our Siena, comes, as we could wish, in private."

He then said to Octavio, "Noble sir!"

Octavio said, "My bosom's secretary, my dearest, best-loved nephew!"

Secretaries know their lord's secrets. Troylo-Savelli knew much about Octavio.

Troylo-Savelli said, "We've been thirsty — eager — in our pursuit."

The pursuit apparently had been of a person such as Livio — and Castamela.

Troylo-Savelli continued, "Sir, here's a gentleman worthy of your knowledge, and as covetous of entertainment — employment — from it. You shall honor your judgment to entrust him to your favors. His merits will commend it."

Livio had just arrived at the court, and he needed gainful employment.

Octavio said to Livio, "You are gladly welcome. Your own worth is a herald to proclaim it. For taste of your preferment, we admit you the chief provisor of our horse."

Livio's new job was to be in charge of Octavio's horses. (In this society, the word "horse" was sometimes a collective plural.) He would be a VIP manager, not a stable boy.

Livio said, "Your bounty makes me your servant forever."

Troylo-Savelli whispered to Octavio, "He's our own. Surely, indeed, most persuadably."

He was saying that Livio would be loyal to Octavio and to him.

"My thanks, sir, I owe to you for this just engagement," Troylo-Savelli said out loud.

He had asked Octavio to hire Livio, and so now he was thanking him for it.

Octavio said to Livio, "Waste no time in entering on your fortunes."

He then said to Troylo-Savelli, "Thou are careful, my Troylo, in the study of a duty."

This was a compliment to his nephew.

Octavio then asked out loud, "His name is ...?"

Troylo-Savelli answered, "Livio."

Livio said, "My name is Livio, my good lord."

Octavio said to Livio, "Again, you're welcome to us."

He said to Troylo-Savelli, "Be as speedy, dear nephew, as thou are constant, steadfast, and faithful. Men of parts, fit parts and sound, are rarely to be met with. But being met with, they therefore are to be cherished with love and with support.

"While I stand, Livio can no way fall. Yet once more, welcome!"

The verb "stand" can mean "have an erection." If Livio really were pandering his sister, Octavio could be understood as saying that as long as Livio's sister sexually excited him, Livio would be prosperous.

Octavio exited.

Troylo-Savelli said, "An honorable liberality, timely disposed without delay or question, commands gratitude."

Livio had quickly been given a respectable position, and he ought to be grateful and loyal on account of it.

A Latin proverb stated, *Bis das, si cito bis.*

Translated: You give twice, if you give quickly.

Troylo-Savelli continued, "Isn't this better than waiting three or four months at livery — with the servants — with cap doffed and knee bent to this chair of state and to that painted arras — wall hanging — for a nod from the goodman-usher, aka doorkeeper, or the formal secretary, and especially the juggler with the purse, who pays some shares in all?"

In other words: Isn't it better to get a position quickly from the head man himself than to wait three or four months among servants to get something worthwhile from one of the higher-ranking servants?

In a way, though, Livio was at livery. He was in charge of Octavio's horses now, and livery was food and provisions for horses as well as food and provisions for servants.

Troylo-Savelli continued, "A younger brother, sometimes an elder, not well trimmed in the headpiece, may spend what his friend — kinsman — left, in expectation of being turned out of service for attendance — that is, dismissed from employment!"

In other words: A foolish person may spend his small inheritance although he suspects that he will soon be out of a job.

This is an example of being downwardly mobile.

Troylo-Savelli continued, "Or he may marry a waiting-woman, and be damned for it to open laughter, and, what's worse, old beggary!"

In other words: A non-wealthy person who marries a waiting-woman instead of a rich woman will be damned and will be impoverished.

This is another example of being downwardly mobile.

Troylo-Savelli then asked, "What thinks my Livio of this rise at first? Is it not miraculous?"

Livio had just arrived at the palace, and he already had a position.

An intelligent man, Livio said, "It seems the bargain was made between you two even before I arrived."

Troylo-Savelli said, "It was, and nothing could void it but the peevish resolution of your dissent on the basis of goodness, as you call it: a thin, threadbare honesty, a virtue without a living to it."

A cynical man, Troylo-Savelli was saying that for Livio to thrive, he must not be good.

An intelligent man, Livio said, "I must resolve to make my sister a whore? I must speak a good word to my sister on behalf of my old bachelor lord — Octavio? Ha! Isn't it so? That is a trifle in respect of present means. Here's all."

Livio was willing to speak that good word to his sister.

Livio's sister could become Octavio's wife — or his mistress.

Livio was OK with being corrupted. After all, he was already being rewarded for it.

Troylo-Savelli replied, "Be yet more confident; the slavery of such an abject office shall not tempt the freedom of thy spirit. Stand ingenious to thine own fate, and we will practice wisely without the charge of scandal."

Pandering one's sister is an abject office — a despicable deed. Yet Livio could work hard in doing that, and he and Troylo-Savelli could accomplish the pandering without causing a scandal.

Livio said, "May it prove to turn out so!"

Secco used a casting-bottle to sprinkle his hat and face with perfumed water, and he carried a little mirror on his belt. He was making himself smell and look good. Secco was Octavio's barber, and the casting-bottle and mirror were tools of his trade.

Secco looked in the mirror and said, "Admirable! Incomparably admirable! To be the minion, the darling, the delight of love — it is a very tickling to the marrow, a kissing in the blood, a bosoming of the ecstasy, the rapture of virginity, the soul and paradise of perfection! Ah, it is pity of generation, Secco, that there are no more such men as you!"

Spadone, one of Octavio's servants, entered the scene.

He loudly announced, "Oyez!"

This was an order to pay attention. It came from the French word for "Hear!"

Spadone, who was seeking Secco, continued, "If any man, woman, or beast, have found, stolen, or taken up a fine, very fine male barber, of the age of above or under eighteen, more or less —"

Secco interrupted, "Spadone, stop! What's the noise?"

"Umph!" Spadone grunted. "Pay the crier. I have been almost lost myself in seeking you. Here's a letter from —"

Secco interrupted, "From whom, whom, my dear Spadone? From whom?"

Spadone said, "Speak softly and fairly! If you are so short with me, I'll return it from where it came, or find a new owner of the letter."

He cried loudly, "Oyez!"

Secco said, "Speak quietly! Quietly! What do thou mean? Is it from the glory of beauty, the fairest of the fair? Be gentle to me. Here's a ducat — speak quietly, please."

Spadone said, "Give me the ducat, and take the letter. It is from the party you mentioned."

They exchanged items.

Spadone continued, "It is golden news — believe it."

Secco said, "Honest Spadone! Divine Morosa!"

He began to read the letter silently.

Spadone said to himself, "Fairest of the fair, you said?

"So is an old rotten pampered mongrel, part-bawd, part-midwife. All the enamel is quite out of her mouth; not the stump of a tooth is left in her head to mumble — eat slowly — the curd of a posset."

A posset is a medicinal drink that is made with hot milk curdled by an alcoholic liquor and spiced and/or sweetened.

Spadone said out loud, "Seignior, it is as I told you; all's right."

"Seignior" is an Italian word meaning "Mister."

Secco replied, "Right, just as thou told me; all's right."

Spadone said, "To a very hair, Seignior *mio*."

Mio is an Italian word meaning "my" or "of mine."

Secco said, "For which, Sirrah Spadone, I will make thee a man; a man, do thou hear? I say, a man."

Spadone, who was rumored to be a eunuch, was insulted.

He said, "Thou are a prick-eared foist, a cittern-headed gewgaw, a knack, a snipper-snapper."

A "foist" is a thief. A prick-eared thief is a good thief — that is, one who has not yet been caught. A crop-eared thief is a thief whose ears have been cropped — the tops have been cut off.

Citterns were stringed musical instruments, the headstock of which was often decorated with a carving of a grotesque face or head.

A gewgaw is a trifle.

A knack is a conman.

A snipper-snapper is a conceited young man.

Spadone said, "Twit me with the decrement of my pendants — the loss of my testicles! Although I am made a gelding, and like a tame buck, have lost my dowsets, aka balls, and although I am more a monster than a cuckold with his horns seen, yet I scorn to be jeered at by any checker-approved barbarian of you all. Make me a man! I defy thee."

Cuckolds were men with unfaithful wives. Cuckolds were supposed to have invisible horns growing out of their heads.

A checker was a checkerboard that served as the sign of a tavern. Spadone was saying that Secco frequented taverns, apparently to an excessive extent.

"Barbarian" was a play on "barber."

Secco said, "How are you now, fellow, how are you now! Ripe for roaring indeed!"

As a person who delivered messages, Spadone frequently cried, "Oyez."

"Indeed!" Spadone said. "Thou are worse: Thou are a dry shaver, a copper-basined suds-monger."

No barber ought to be a dry shaver.

Secco said, "Nay, nay; by my mistress' fair eyes, I meant no such thing."

He was saying that he had been misunderstood. "I'll make you a man" was not a reference to Spadone's rumored lack of testicles.

Spadone said, "Eyes in thy belly! The reverend madam shall know how I have been treated. I will blow my nose in thy casting-bottle, break the teeth of thy combs, poison thy camphor-balls, slice thy towels with thine own razor, put tallow on thy tweezers, and pee urine in thy basin — make me a man!"

Secco said, "Hold on, take another ducat. As I love new clothes —"

Spadone interrupted, "Or cast aside old ones."

Secco said, "Yes, or cast aside old ones, I intended no insult to you."

Taking the money, Spadone said, "Good, we are pieced together again."

By becoming friends again, they were pieced together and at peace with each other.

He continued, "Reputation, Seignior, is precious."

"I know it is," Secco replied.

"Old sores don't want to be rubbed," Spadone said.

Secco said, "In my opinion, they ought never to be rubbed."

Spadone said, "The lady guardian, the 'mother' of the three Fancies, is resolved to draw with you in the wholesome yoke of matrimony quickly."

The lady guardian was Secco's beloved: Morosa. She was the guardian of the Fancies: three young and pretty women.

Secco replied, "She writes as much, and, Spadone, when we are married —"

Spadone interrupted, "You will go to bed, no doubt."

Secco said, "We will revel in such variety of delights —"

Spadone interrupted, "— do miracles, and get babies."

Since Morosa was an old woman, her becoming pregnant would be a miracle.

Secco continued, "— live so sumptuously —"

Spadone interrupted, "— in feather and old furs."

Secco continued, "— feed so deliciously —"

Spadone interrupted, "— on pap and bull-beef."

"Pap" is semi-liquid food, suitable for an old woman.

"Pap and bull-beef" can also be understood as Morosa's breast and Secco's penis.

Secco continued, "— enjoy the sweetness of our years —"

Spadone interrupted, "— eighteen and threescore with advantage."

Secco was eighteen years old; Morosa was over sixty years old.

Secco continued, "— tumble and wallow in such abundance —"

Spadone interrupted, "— the pure crystal puddle of pleasures."

Secco continued, "— that all the world would wonder."

Spadone said, "A pox on them who envy you!"

Secco asked, "How are the beauties, my dainty knave? How do they live, wish, think, and dream, sirrah, ha!"

The beauties were the three Fancies.

Spadone said, "They fumble one with another on the skips and leaps of imagination between their legs; they do eat and sleep, play games, laugh, and lie down, as beauties ought to do. That's all."

One animal such as a horse will "leap" on another in order to have sex with it.

A "skip" is an act of passing from one thing to another. In sex, a little something passes from the man to the woman.

To "fumble" is to "use the fingers" awkwardly. This kind of fumbling appears to be mutual masturbation.

Secco said, "Commend me to my choicest, Morosa, and tell her the minute of her appointment shall be waited on; say to her that she shall find me a man at all points."

"At all points" meant "at all times" and "at all appointments."

An erect penis also points.

Spadone said, "Why, there's another quarrel — you said 'man' once more, in spite of my nose!"

A long nose can be likened to a penis.

Nitido, Octavio's page, entered the room and said, "Leave here, Secco, leave! My lord calls for you. He has a loose hair that has moved away from its fellows; a clip of your art is commanded."

Secco the barber said, "I now fly there, Nitido."

"Spadone, remember me."

Secco exited.

Nitido said, "Trudging between an old mule and a young calf, my nimble intelligencer?'

The old mule was Morosa, and the young calf was Secco. A mule is a woman: The Latin word *mulier* means woman. A calf is a fool.

Nitido, however, stumbled while pronouncing a word, and he may have said "moyle" instead of "mule." A moyle is a tumult. Perhaps he meant that Morosa was or would be a quarrelsome old woman.

Nitido then asked, "What, thou fatten apace on capon still?"

A capon is a castrated cock.

Insulted, Spadone said, "Yes, crimp."

"Crimp" was a derogatory term. Possibly it was a portmanteau word combining "criminal" and "pimp."

Spadone continued, referring to Nitido's supposed occupation, "It is a gallant life to be an old lord's pimp-whiskin."

A whiskin is a pander. The old lord is Octavio.

Spadone continued, "But beware of the porter's lodge for carrying tales out of the school."

The porter's lodge was where unruly servants were punished. Nitido could get in trouble if he told tales about Octavio's supposed immoral sexual activities.

Nitido said, "What a terrible sight to a libbed — castrated — breech, aka crotch, is a sow-gelder!"

A sow-gelder spays sows. The word "geld" means to deprive of an important part.

Spadone replied, "Not so terrible a sight as is a cross-tree that never grows to a wag-halter page."

A cross-tree that never grows is a gallows.

A "wag-halter page" is a witty page who is destined to hang by a noose from a gallows.

Nitido said, "Good! Witty rascal, thou are a Satyr, I admit, except that the nymphs need not fear the evidence of thy mortality."

The nymphs are the three Fancies.

Human mortals are either male or female, but a castrated man lacks some evidence of being male.

Nitido continued, "Go, put on a clean bib, and spin among the nuns, sing them a bawdy song. All the children thou beget shall be christened in wassail-bowls, and turned into a college of men-midwives."

Wassail-bowls are filled with wine or ale, not with holy water.

Nitido continued, "Farewell, nightmare!"

"Very, very well," Spadone said. "If I die in thy debt for this, crack-rope, let me be buried in a coal-sack. I'll fit you, ape's-face! Look for it."

A crack-rope is a rogue who is likely to die on a gallows.

An ape-face is ugly.

Nitido sang, "*And still the urchin would, but could not do.*"

An urchin is a boy.

A castrated man would — wants to — have sex but cannot.

"Do" means "have sex."

Spadone said, "Mark the end of it, and laugh at last."

Spadone intended to have the last laugh.

— 1.3 —

Romanello and Castamela talked in a room in Livio's house. Castamela was Livio's sister, and Romanello wanted to marry her.

Romanello said, "Tell me you cannot love me."

Castamela replied, "You importune too strict a resolution. As you are a gentleman of commendable qualities and fair deserts in every sweet condition that becomes a hopeful promise, I do honor the example — the model of perfection — of your youth; but, sir, our fortunes, concluded on both sides in narrow bands, move you to construe gently my forbearance in argument of fit consideration."

Neither of them had much wealth, and that was reason enough for them not to marry. Romanello need not believe that she did not love him. She, Castamela, could want him to marry a woman who would bring wealth to him.

Romanello said, "Why, Castamela, I have shaped thy virtues, even from our childish years, into a dowry of richer estimation than thy portion doubled a hundred times can equal."

According to Romanello, Castamela's dowry was her virtues, which were worth much more than mere money.

He continued, "Now I clearly find thy current of affection labors to fall into the gulf of riot, not the free ocean of a soft content."

He was accusing her of preferring to marry into money so that she could enjoy riotous living.

Romanello continued, "You'd marry pomp and plenty. It is the idol, I must confess, that creatures of the time bend their devotions to; but I have fashioned thoughts much more excellent of you."

He had believed that she was better than this.

Castamela said, "Enjoy your own prosperity."

She meant that he could enjoy whatever prosperity he had without her.

She continued, "I am resolved never by any charge with me to force poverty upon you, want of love."

Marrying him and making herself his responsibility would make him poor, and she was determined not to make him poor.

As for Romanello, she called him "want of love." By his wanting to marry her, a woman who could not bring him a good dowry of wealth, he was showing a lack of responsibility. A man who truly loved a woman would make sure that he would not fall into poverty and so make his wife poor.

Castamela continued, "Want of love is rarely cherished with the love of want."

The love of want is the love of voluntary poverty. Those who embrace voluntary poverty are often religious people who do not want — lack — love because they love and are loved by God. Such people tend to be priests and nuns who do not marry in a secular sense.

Love is of different kinds. Love of God can lead one to embrace voluntary poverty. Love of a mortal woman ought not to lead one to embrace voluntary poverty: Money is needed to provide for one's family.

Castamela finished, "I'll not be your undoing."

She would not make Romanello poor by marrying him instead of allowing him to marry a rich woman.

Romanello said, "Surely, some dotage of living stately and richly lends a cunning to eloquence. How this piece of goodness is changed to ambition! Oh, you are most miserable in your desires! The female curse has caught you."

He was saying that she had changed — for the worse. Her mental faculties had been impaired, and now she was pursuing wealth.

Castamela said, "Bah! Bah! How ill this suits you!"

His criticism of her was making him look bad.

Angry, Romanello said, "A devil of pride ranges in airy thoughts to catch a star, while you grasp molehills."

Castamela said, "You are worse and worse, I vow."

Romanello said, "Except that some remnant of an honest sense ebbs a full tide of blood to shame, all women would prostitute all honor to the luxury of ease and titles."

He was accusing all women of being prone to seek to marry wealthy and titled men. Only some small sense of honor kept them from doing that.

Castamela said, "Romanello, know that you have forgotten the nobleness of truth and are fixated on scandal now."

Romanello said, "A dog, a parrot, a monkey, a luxurious coach known as a caroche, a richly clothed lackey, a waiting-woman with her lips sealed up, are pretty toys to please my Mistress Wanton!"

A "waiting-woman with her lips sealed up" is one who will tell no tales of wifely adultery.

He continued, "So is a fiddle, too; a fiddle will make Mistress Wanton dance, or else be sick and whine."

Castamela said, "This is uncivil. I am not, sir, your charge."

She was not his responsibility — or his financial burden.

Romanello said, "It is to my grief that you are, for all my services are lost and ruined."

She was his source of trouble — his charge or burden — for she was rejecting all the wooing that he had done of her.

Castamela said, "This is my chief opinion of your worthiness, when such distractions as these you speak of tempt you: You would prove to be a cruel lord, who dares, being yet a wooer of me, as you profess, to criticize my best respects of duty to your welfare; it is a madness I have not often observed."

She had been trying to show consideration for him, believing as she did that it would be best for him to acquire wealth rather than marry her. All she had received for her consideration were insults.

She continued, "Possess your freedom. You have no right in me. Let this suffice: I wish your joys much comfort."

Livio, wearing rich clothing, entered the room.

He said to Castamela, "Sister, see how, by a new creation of my tailor's, I've shaken off old mortality."

Mortality is death or disease. Livio's fancy new clothing had shaken off the "disease" of poverty.

He continued, "The rags of home-spun gentry — please, sister, observe it — are cast aside, and I now appear in fashion to men, and I am approved by them. Observe me, sister. The consequence concerns you."

Castamela said, "That is true, good brother, for my well-doing must consist in yours."

His rising higher in social status meant that Castamela could meet and might marry a man of higher social status than she would have otherwise.

Livio said, "Here's Romanello, a fine-tempered gallant, of decent bodily bearing, of indifferent means, considering that his sister, newly hoist up from a lost merchant's warehouse to the titles of a great lord's bed, may supply his wants ..."

Romanello's sister was Flavia, who was separated from a poor merchant and who had married Julio de Varana, a wealthy lord of Camerino, Italy. Julio had the wealth to supply Romanello — his brother-in-law — with what he needed. Romanello's sister could encourage Julio to do that.

He continued, "... not sunk in his acquaintance, for a scholar able enough, and one who may subsist without the help of friends, provided always he does not fly upon wedlock without the certainty of an advancement. As long as he does not marry, a bachelor may thrive by frugality on a little."

Romanello was a scholar and could support himself. But if he were to marry without getting a good position or without getting a dowry, then he — and his wife — would not be able to subsist without the help of friends.

Livio continued, "A single life's no burden; but to draw in yokes is chargeable and will require a double maintenance."

If Romanello were to be yoked in marriage to Castamela, his expenses would go way up.

Livio continued, "Why, I can live without a wife and purchase."

"Purchase" is annual income from property. Such property may make up a wife's dowry.

Or Livio said, "Why, I can live without a wife, and purchase."

If that is what he said, then he meant that he could live without a wife and could purchase an estate.

Romanello said, "Is this a mystery you've lately found out, Livio, or a cunning concealed until now for wonder?"

Romanello had seen Livio's new clothes. How had he acquired them? Had he recently learned how to acquire wealth, or had he simply kept his knowledge a secret until now so he could shock his sister with his finery?

Livio said, "Bah! Believe it: Endeavors and an active brain are better than patrimonies left by parents."

According to Livio's words, energetic action and intelligence are better than patrimonies: wealth, name, titles, and family reputation.

Did he believe this?

Livio continued, "Find it out by experience.

"One man thrives by cheating; cheating knaves fly at shallow fools and unthrifty people and spendthrifts and make them their game — their victims.

"Then a fellow relies on his hair — his strength, as in the story of Samson — and that his back can toil for fodder from the city.

"These are lies."

Con men can prosper, but they often go through fallow periods.

A strong man can sell his labor to a city government and make enough to buy food, but strong men grow old and weak.

Livio continued, "Another man, reputed to be valiant, lives by the sword, and takes up quarrels, or braves them, as the novice likes, to gild the novice's reputation.

"This is most improbable: It is not easy to believe."

At this time, young men who were known as roaring boys quarreled and fought with each other. Many people, including playwrights, regarded the roaring boys poorly and as bullies.

Reputedly, a man who was thought to be brave could educate a novice in the practice of quarreling, and if paid enough, would quarrel with the novice and deliberately lose to him, thus making the novice look valiant.

Livio continued, "A world of desperate undertakings possibly procures some hungry meals, aka meals that are eagerly and hungrily eaten; some tavern-surfeits, aka times of drunkenness; and some frippery, aka tawdry finery, to hide nakedness.

"Perhaps scrambling successfully procures half a ducat now and then so he can roar and noise it with the tattling hostess for a week's lodging.

"These are pretty shifts that souls bankrupt of their royalty submit to.

"Give me a man whose practice and experience conceives not barely the philosopher's stone, but indeed has it; give me one whose wit's his Indies."

Livio was praising men who could live well by their wits. The alchemists' philosopher's stone was supposed to turn base metals into silver and gold. The Indies were renowned for their wealth. One meaning of the word "practice" is trickery, and many alchemists were tricksters who defrauded fools into giving up good money to acquire something that did not and could never exist.

Not all men can live well by their wits. These men include those whom Livio spoke of above.

Livio was not against cheats; he was against unsuccessful cheats.

He believed that it would be much better to pander your sister to a rich man than to be a poor cheat.

Livio continued, "The poor are most ridiculous."

Did Livio argue that energetic action and intelligence are better than patrimonies? If he had attempted to do so, he had not proven the point.

Most likely, Livio would have preferred to be born wealthy. Since he had not, he was pretending to prefer another way of acquiring wealth: pandering his sister.

Romanello said, "You're pleasant in new discoveries of fortune. Use them with moderation, Livio."

"You're pleasant" meant "You're making jokes."

Castamela, Livio's sister, said, "Such wild language used to be a stranger to your customary way of speaking. However, brother, you are pleased to vent it, but I hope you do so for recreation and don't mean it."

Livio said, "Name and honor — what are they? A mere sound without supportance."

"Supportance" means 1) corroboration and 2) sustenance.

Livio continued, "A begging chastity, youth, beauty, handsomeness, discourse, behavior that might charm attention and curse the gazer's eyes into amazement — these are nature's common bounties.

"Nature's bounties are also uncut diamonds, unworn flowers, unwrought silkworms' webs, and unrefined gold.

"All those glories are of esteem when used and given a price.

"There's no dark sense in this."

Livio was saying that nothing is valuable or valued until it can be used and is given a price.

Romanello said, "I don't understand the drift of your conversation, or how you mean it, or even to whom you are directing it."

Castamela said, "Please, brother, speak more plainly."

Livio said, "First, Romanello, I say this for your satisfaction:

"If you waste more hours in courtship to this maiden, my sister, weighing her competency — her wealth — with your own, you go about to build without foundation, so that care will prove void."

In other words: You are wasting your time wooing my sister because she can't make you rich.

Romanello said, "A sure acquittance, if I must be discharged."

He was punning, darkly. An acquittance is 1) a release from debt, and 2) a release from trouble. A debt can be discharged, but a person who is discharged is banned from doing something — such as wooing Castamela.

Romanello would escape the burden of supporting a family if he did not marry Castamela.

Livio said, "Next, Castamela, to thee, my own beloved sister, let me say that I have not been so bountiful in showing to fame the treasure that this age has opened as thy true value merits."

He had not been making known to others his sister's merits. Those others would include high-ranking men who would woo her.

Castamela said, "You are merry."

In other words: You are joking.

Livio said, "My solicitude for the protection of thy fresh-blooming years prompted a fear of tending too cautiously thy growth to such perfection as no flattery of art can destroy now."

Her beauty now would shine through makeup. Her innocence would now remain even in the face of skillful flattery.

Castamela said, "Here's talk in riddles! Brother, what is the meaning of your words?"

Livio said, "I'll no longer chamber thy freedom. We have been already thrifty enough in our low fortunes; henceforth, command thy liberty, and with thy liberty command thy pleasures."

In other words: Castamela was free to go to social events and have fun. By so doing, she would be able to meet a rich man.

Romanello said, "Has it come to this?"

Castamela said to her brother, "You're wondrously full of courtesy."

He was giving her very much freedom very, very quickly.

Livio said, "Ladies of birth and quality are suitors for being known to you: They want to be introduced to you and know you socially. I have promised, sister, that they shall partake of your company."

Castamela asked, "What ladies? Where, when, how, who?"

Livio answered, "A day, a week, a month sported — spent in enjoying entertainments — among such beauties is a gain on time; they're young, wise, noble, fair, and chaste."

Castamela asked, "Chaste?"

Livio replied, "Yes, Castamela, chaste. I would not hazard my hopes, my joys of thee on a dangerous trial."

He was saying that he did not want to expose her to bad influences.

He continued, "Yet if, as it may chance, a neat-clothed merriment should pass without blush in tattling, so long as the words fall not too broadly, it is only a pastime smiled at among yourselves in private; but beware of being overheard."

A neat-clothed merriment is a well-expressed merry comment, but also one that is expressed by a well-dressed person such as Octavio.

Castamela said, sarcastically, "This is pretty!"

Romanello said to himself, "I fear something, but I don't know what it is yet, and so I must be silent."

Troylo-Savelli entered the room. With him were the three Fancies: Floria, Clarella, and Silvia. Also with him was Nitido, Octavio's page.

Livio said, "They come as soon as spoken of.

"Sweetest fair ones, my sister cannot but conceive this to be a special honor in your respects. This honor is special because it comes particularly from you."

He then said to Troylo-Savelli, "Dear sir, you grace us in your favors."

Troylo-Savelli said to Castamela, "Virtuous lady!"

Floria said, "We are your servants."

Clarella said, "We are your sure friends."

Silvia said, "Society may fix us in a league."

By spending time together, they could very well become a band of four. Right now, the three Fancies were a band of three.

Castamela said, "All of you are appropriately welcome.

"I find no reason, gentle ladies, whereon to cast this debt of mine."

The debt was social.

Castamela's words were ambiguous. She could be saying that she didn't deserve such attention, or she could be saying that the three Fancies had no good reason to visit her.

The word "appropriately" was also ambiguous. Which welcome was appropriate depended on the meaning of "I find no reason, gentle ladies, whereon to cast this debt of mine."

Castamela continued, "But my acknowledgment shall study out a way to pay my thankfulness to you."

Troylo-Savelli said to her, "Sweet beauty, your brother has indeed been too much a churl in this concealment from us all, who love him, of such a desired presence. He did wrong in hiding you from us."

Silvia said, "Please enrich us with your wished-for amity. We want to be friends with you."

Floria said, "Our coach waits for us. We cannot be denied."

She was saying that they would not take no for an answer: They really wanted Castamela to come with them for a social visit.

Clarella said, "Command the coach, Nitido."

In other words: Command that the coach driver be ready to drive them away at once.

Nitido said, "Ladies, I shall."

As he exited, he said to himself, "Now for a lusty harvest! It will prove to be a cheap year, should these barns once be filled."

Knowing Nitido, he was using the word "barns" to mean "vaginas."

When many vaginas are filled and then emptied, the laws of the marketplace dictate that finding a vagina to fill will be easy and the vagina will be cheap.

Castamela said, "Brother, one word in private."

Livio said to himself, "Phew! Soon I shall instruct you at large."

He meant that soon he would be able to speak to her clearly and tell her what to do.

He said out loud, and not in private, "We are prepared, and easily persuaded. It is good manners not to be troublesome."

Troylo-Savelli said, "Thou are perfect, Livio. You said exactly the right thing."

Castamela asked, "To where are we going?"

She thought to herself, *But he's my brother. I must go.*

Troylo-Savelli said to her, "Fair lady, give me your arm. I am your usher, lady."

Giving him her arm, Castamela said, "As you please, sir."

Livio said, "I will escort you to your coach."

He said to Romanello, "Some two hours from now I shall return again."

Everyone except Romanello exited.

Romanello said to himself:

"Troylo-Savelli is the next heir to the Marquis!

"And the page, too, was the Marquis' own page!

"Livio has been transformed into a man suddenly wearing splendid clothing, and he has altered in his nature, or I dream! He has changed!

"Among the ladies, I don't remember that I have seen one face.

"There's cunning in these changes: I am resolute either to pursue the trickery involved in them, or to lose my labor."

If he did not find out what was going on, it would not be for lack of trying.

CHAPTER 2

— 2.1 —

Flavia, accompanied by Camillo and Vespucci, entered an apartment in Julio's house. Flavia was Romanello's sister; she had recently married the wealthy lord Julio. Camillo and Vespucci were Julio's attendants.

"He has not yet returned?" Flavia asked.

"Madam?" Camillo asked.

"The lord our husband we mean," Flavia said. "He is unkind! Four hours are almost past, with only twelve short minutes lacking by the sandglass, since we broke company. There was never, gentlemen, a poor princess treated like this!"

Vespucci said, "With your gracious favor, peers, great in rank and place, ought of necessity to attend to state-employments."

Camillo said, "For such duties are all their toil and labor; but their pleasures flow in the beauties they enjoy, which conquer all sense of other travail."

"That is trimly spoken," Flavia said. "When we were common, mortal, and a subject, as other creatures of Heaven's making are, the more the pity, bless us, how we waited for the huge play-day — the Lord-Mayor's day — when the pageant-flags fluttered about the city, for we then were certain the madam-courtiers would condescend to visit us, and call us by our names, and eat our food. Indeed, they would give us permission to sit at the upper end of our own tables, telling us how welcome they'd make us when we came to court.

"Very little dreamed I at that time of the wind that blew me up to the weathercock of the honors that now are thrust upon me, but we'll bear the burden, even if it were twice as much as it is.

"The next great feast we'll grace the city-wives — the poor souls — and see how they'll behave themselves before our presence. You two shall wait on us."

"With the best observance and with the best glory in our service," Vespucci said.

"We are creatures made proud in your commands," Camillo said.

Flavia said, "I believe that you are so, and you shall find us readier in your pleasures than you in your obedience.

"Bah! I think that I am in an excellent mood to be pettish, a little toysome: whimsical and playful. It is a pretty sign of breeding, isn't it, sirs? I could, indeed, long for some strange good things now."

"Such news, madam, would overjoy my lord your husband," Camillo said.

"Command bonfires and bell-ringings," Vespucci said.

Flavia said, "I must be with child, then, if it be just for the public jollity, or lose my longings, which would be a mighty pity."

She was saying — not seriously — that only a pregnant woman would have such longings.

"May the sweet fates forbid it!" Camillo said.

Fabricio entered the room. He was Flavia's first husband, and he was an unsuccessful merchant.

He said, "Noblest lady —"

Vespucci interrupted, "Rudeness! Keep off, or I shall — saucy groom, learn manners. Go swab among your goblins."

A "groom" is a "servant," and "to swab" means "to behave rudely."

"Let him stay," Flavia ordered. "The fellow I have seen, and I now remember his name: Fabricio."

The word "fellow" was often used to address a man of lower social status than the speaker. Often, the word was used derogatively.

Fabricio said, "I am your poor creature, lady. Out of your gentleness, may it please you to consider the contents of this petition, which contains all hope of my last fortunes."

He was asking for something because he was desperately needy.

Flavia said, "Give me the petition."

Camillo took the petition from Fabricio and gave it to Flavia, saying, "Here, madam."

Flavia walked a short distance away and read the petition.

Camillo then said quietly, "Notice, Vespucci, how the wittol stares at his former wife."

A cuckold is a man with an unfaithful wife. A wittol is a cuckold who doesn't mind his wife cheating on him.

Camillo continued, quietly, "Surely, he imagines that to be a cuckold by consent is purchase of approbation in a state."

In other words: Surely, he believed that allowing himself to be cuckolded is a way to purchase the approval of a powerful man.

Vespucci said, "He has good reason to believe that. The gain reprieved him from a bankrupt's statute, and it filed him in the charter of his freedom."

By allowing Julio to marry his wife, Fabricio had received money that got him out of bankruptcy and bought his freedom.

Camillo continued, quietly, "She said that she had seen the fellow before — the fellow is her former husband! Did you notice?"

"I noticed it most punctually," Camillo whispered. "She could call him by his name, too!"

He then whispered, cynically, "Why, is it possible she has not yet forgotten he was her husband?"

Vespucci whispered back, cynically, "That would be strange."

Perhaps they really believed that a woman whose marriage to a poor man had been invalidated and who had then married a rich man would very quickly forget, or pretend to forget, being married to the poor man.

Vespucci then whispered, "Oh, she is a precious trinket! Has a puppet ever so slipped up?"

He believed that Flavia had messed up: She would have done much better to pretend not to know or recognize her former husband.

Camillo whispered, "The tale of Venus' cat, man, changed into a woman, was an emblem but to this."

Can a living being change its nature? The god Jupiter and the goddess Venus disagreed: Jupiter thought that a living being could change its nature, but Venus thought that it could not. To find out who was right, Jupiter changed a cat into a young woman and gave her to a young man to marry. The young woman sat demurely on a chair. Jupiter said, "See! A living being can change its nature." Venus took a mouse she had earlier put in her pocket and released it. The young woman jumped off the chair and pounced on the mouse. Venus said, "See! A living being cannot change its nature."

Camillo was arguing that human beings cannot change their nature. If Flavia could change her nature, then as a woman married to a rich man she would not have recognized her husband: She would have forgotten him by now.

Camillo continued, "She turns toward him."

Vespucci said, "He stands just like Actaeon in the painted tapestry."

Actaeon was an ancient Greek hunter who saw the goddess Artemis bathing naked in a stream while he was hunting deer. Artemis is a militant virgin. Not pleased that Actaeon had seen her naked, she turned him into a horned stag and his own dogs chased him down and killed him. Because of the horns on Actaeon's head, he was later associated with cuckoldry and earned the name of cuckold. Cuckolds have unfaithful wives, and depictions of cuckolds show them with horns on their head.

Camillo said, "Say no more. Let's be quiet."

Flavia said, "Friend, we have read and weighed the sum of what your scrivener — your scribe — which in effect is meant your learned counsel, has drawn for you."

She was saying that instead of having legal counsel write the letter, he had had only a scribe write the letter. No doubt he could not afford legal counsel.

She continued, "It is a fair hand, indeed, but the contents are somewhat unseasonable; for, let us tell you, you've been a spender, a vain spender. You have wasted your stock of credit and of wares unthriftily. You are a faulty man; and should we urge our lord as often for supplies as shame or wants drive you to ask, it might be construed as an impudence — which we defy — an impudence, base in base women, but sinful in noble women.

"Aren't you ashamed yet of yourself?"

This was not the first time that he had come to her to beg for money.

Fabricio said, "Great lady, I'm ashamed of my misfortunes."

Camillo whispered to Vespucci, "So, so! This jeer twangs roundly, doesn't it, Vespucci? Her insult resounds harshly!"

Vespucci whispered to Camillo, "Why, here's a worshipful lady! Here's a lady we can respect!"

Flavia said to Camillo and Vespucci, "Please, gentlemen, retire for a while. This fellow shall resolve some doubts that stick about me."

Camillo and Vespucci said, "As you please."

They exited.

Flavia said, "To thee, Fabricio — oh, the change is cruel — since I find some small leisure and opportunity to talk to you, I must affirm that thou are unworthy of the name of man.

"Those holy marriage vows that we, by bonds of faith, recorded in the register of truth, were kept by me unbroken; no assaults of gifts, of courtship, from the great and wanton, no threats or sense of poverty, to which thy riotous behavior had betrayed me, could betray my warrantable — good, true, and genuine — thoughts to impure folly.

"Why would thou force me to be miserable?"

Although her then-husband had been a spendthrift and had reduced both himself and her to poverty, she had always remained faithful and loyal to him.

Fabricio replied, "The scorn of rumor is reward enough to brand my lewder actions: It was, I thought, impossible that a beauty fresh as was your youth could endure the last of my decays."

His decays were bad behavior that resulted in impoverishment. The last of his decays could be forthcoming old age.

"Did I complain?" Flavia replied. "My sleeps between thine arms were even as sound, my dreams as harmless, my happiness as free, as when the best of plenty crowned our bride-bed.

"Among some of a mean but quiet fortune, distrust of what they call their own, or jealousy of those whom in their bosoms they possess without a need of force or control, begets a self-unworthiness."

Fabricio had believed that he did not deserve such a woman as Flavia.

She said, "Because of this, out of fear, or what is worse, desire of paltry gain, they practice skill, and labor to pander their own wives — those wives, whose innocence, stranger to language, spoke obedience only — and such a wife was Flavia to Fabricio."

Men who believe that they are unworthy of good wives may try to pander those wives — out of fear that they will lose their wife anyway, or simply out of desire for money. They do this to wives who are innocent and obedient, as good wives in this society ought to be. Such wives' innocence is a stranger to language. They behave in such a way that ought not to cause gossip.

Fabricio replied, "My loss is irrecoverable."

He had lost Flavia, and this loss was irrecoverable.

Flavia said, "Don't call thy wickedness thy loss."

He still had his wickedness.

Flavia continued, "Without my knowledge, thou sold me, and in open court thou protested a pre-contract to another falsely, to justify a judicial separation."

Fabricio had taken action to lose Flavia: This was not something that had just happened to happen to him.

He had testified in court that before he married Flavia, a pre-contract had existed. One of them had made an agreement to be married to someone else. He had argued that this pre-contract of marriage invalidated his marriage to her. To Flavia, this was a false invalidation of their marriage.

Why had he done this? For money to get out of bankruptcy. Julio had given him that money to invalidate his marriage to Flavia so that he could marry her.

Flavia continued, "Wherein could I offend, to be believed thy strumpet, in the best sense an adulteress?"

She had done nothing to deserve the name of strumpet or adulteress. Unfortunately, Flavia's marriage to Fabricio had been invalidated, and so she had not been married to him while she was sleeping with him.

She continued, "I am now so thought to be a strumpet or an adulteress now that I have been shaken off even from my own blood. Even my own relatives want nothing to do with me.

"The blood I have is not noble, yet it is not mean.

"As for Romanello, my only brother, he shuns me, and he abhors to acknowledge that I am his sister."

Fabricio said, "It is said that I am the shame of mankind."

This triangle was greatly gossiped about.

Flavia said, "I live happy in this great lord Julio's love now; but if his cunning could have trained me to do the dishonor of committing adultery with him, we would have never been sundered by the temptation of his purchase."

If she had committed adultery with Julio, he would have given her money that she would have given to Fabricio, and her and Fabricio's marriage would never have been invalidated.

Julio may have actually tried to tempt her to commit adultery, or Flavia may be now speaking hypothetically.

Flavia continued, "Truly, Fabricio, I am little proud of my unsought honors and I am so far from feeling triumphant that I am not more fool to such as honor me than to myself, who hate this antic carriage."

Her "antic carriage" was the silly behavior she affected.

Flavia was pretending to enjoy her new, wealthy life, but this was an act that she was putting on for others — an act that she did not enjoy performing.

Fabricio said, "You are an angel rather to be worshipped than grossly to be talked with."

Flavia gave him some money and said, "Keep those ducats. I shall provide you better.

"It would be an act of bravery and fortitude if you could forget the place wherein you've rendered your name forever hateful."

It would be best if he would stop coming to her for money that she was willing to give him although she recognized him for the weak man that he was.

Fabricio said, "I will do it, do it, most excellent goodness, and conclude my days in silent goodness."

He was saying that he would reform.

Flavia said, "You may prosper in Spain, in France, or elsewhere, as in Italy. Besides, you are a bred scholar; however, you interrupted your study with commerce.

"I'll think of your needs and supply them.

"In the meantime, please, don't storm at my behavior to you; I have forgotten acquaintance with my own relatives."

He moved toward her, and she said, "Keep your first distance."

He moved back.

Flavia called, "Camillo! Who is near? Vespucci!"

Julio, her new husband, entered the room, along with Camillo and Vespucci.

Seeing Fabricio, Julio said, "What! Our lady's cast-aside familiar?"

Flavia said, "Oh, my stomach feels nauseous at the sight of — sick, sick, I am sick. I faint at heart."

She said to Julio, "Kiss me. Please, quickly, or I shall faint. You've stayed a sweet while from me."

Referring to Fabricio, she said, "And this companion, too — curse him!"

She said the word "companion" contemptuously.

Julio replied, "Dearest, thou are my health, my blessing."

He ordered, "Throw the bankrupt out of my doors!"

He then said to Fabricio, "Sirrah, I'll have thee whipped, if thou come here again."

Camillo said, "Leave! Get away from here, you vermin!"

Fabricio exited.

Julio asked, "How are you, my best of joys?"

Flavia said, "I am prettily mended, now we have our own lord — you — here. I shall never endure to spare you long out of my sight.

"Look at what the thing presented to me."

The thing was Fabricio.

Flavia gave Fabricio's petition to Julio.

Julio said, "A petition, likely, for some new charity?"

The charity was additional money for Fabricio.

Flavia said, "We must not be troubled with his needs; a wanting creature is monstrous, is as ominous — damn it! Dispatch the silly 'mushroom' once and for all, and send him with some pittance out of the country, where we may hear no more of him."

She used the word "mushroom" ironically. A mushroom is a person who seems to rise overnight, just as a mushroom grows overnight. Fabricio was far from rising.

Julio said, "Thy will shall stand as a law to me, my Flavia."

He would give Fabricio money to leave the country.

Flavia said, "You have been in private conversation with our fellow-peers now. Shall we not know how the business stands? Surely, in some country ladies are privy-counselors, I guarantee you. Aren't they, do you think? There the land is doubtlessly most shrewdly and skillfully governed. All the women wear swords and breeches, I have heard most certainly: Such sights would be excellent."

Julio replied, "Thou are a matchless pleasure. No life is sweet without thee. In my heart reign as empress, and be titled thy Julio's sovereign, my only precious dear."

Flavia said, "We'll prove to be no less to you."

Troylo-Savelli and Livio talked together in a room in the palace.

Livio was feeling jealous, a word that in this culture meant apprehensive of evil.

Troylo-Savelli said, "Sea-sick ashore still! Thou could rarely scape a calenture — fever — in a long voyage, Livio, who in a short one, and at home, are subject to such faint stomach-qualms; no cordials comfort the business of thy thoughts, for anything I see. What ails thee, man? Be merry, hang up jealousies."

Livio said, "Who, I? I jealous? No, no, here's no cause in this place. It is a nunnery, a retirement for meditation; all the difference extant but puzzles only bare belief, not grounds it."

Troylo-Savelli had used the metaphor of a sea-voyage. When Livio used the word "grounds," he was referring to the metaphor of a ship running aground. Livio was saying that at most he was mildly apprehensive, but did he mean it?

Livio continued, "Rich services in gold and silver plate, soft and fair lodgings, varieties of recreations, exercise of music in all changes, elegant servants, princely — no, royal — equipage of garments, satiety of gardens, orchards, waterworks, pictures so ravishing that ranging eyes might dwell upon them into old age without a single wish for livelier substance — the great world in a little world of fancy is here abstracted: no temptation is offered but such as fools and mad folks can invite to."

This kind of invitation is like a bribe: an inducement to do something, such as pander one's own sister.

Livio continued, "And yet —"

Troylo-Savelli interrupted, "And yet your reason cannot answer the objections of your fears, which argue danger."

Livio said, "Danger!

"No, they argue dishonor, Troylo.

"If my sister were safe from those charms, I must confess I could live here forever."

Troylo-Savelli said, "But you could not, I can assure you, for it would then be scarcely possible that a door might open to you — hardly a loophole would open to you."

In other words: Cease pandering your sister, and these doors to wealth and luxury will close to you.

So far, the pandering had consisted of making her available socially. This, however, opened the possibility that a wealthy man might seduce her and make her his mistress.

Livio said, "My presence, then, is the usher to her ruin, and the loss of her is the fruit of my preferment?"

Troylo-Savelli said, "Briefly partake of a secret, but be sure to lodge it in the deepest part of thy bosom, where memory may not find it for discovery. By our firm truth of friendship, I require this of thee."

Livio replied, "By our firm truth of friendship, I agree and subscribe to just conditions."

Troylo-Savelli said, "Our great uncle-Marquis, Octavio, disabled from his cradle by an impotence in nature first, that impotence since seconded and rendered more infirm by a fatal — deadly — wound received in fight against the Turkish galleys, has been made incapable of any faculty of active manhood, more than what affections proper to his sex must else distinguish, so that no helps of skill and art can warrant life, should he transcend the bounds his weakness limits."

In other words: According to Troylo-Savelli, Octavio was sexually impotent. If he were to attempt to have sex, he could die.

Livio said, "Go on. I am listening with eagerness."

Troylo-Savelli said, "It is strange that such natural defects at no time check a full and free sufficiency of spirit, which flows both in so clear and fixed a strength, that to confirm belief, it seems, where nature is in the body lame, she is supplied in fine proportion of the mind.

"A word concludes all. To a man who is his enemy, he is dangerous and threatening, but to women, however pleasurable, he is in no way able to show the abilities of love, other than what his outward senses can delight in, or expense and generosity court with."

Troylo-Savelli was saying that despite Octavio's being sexually impotent, he appeared to be a masculine, dangerous, and threatening man to his enemies. He was able to give gifts to the ladies, but unable to bed them.

Livio said, "Good, good, Troylo. Oh, I wish that I had a lusty faith to credit it, although none of all this wonder should be possible!"

Could be believe what Troylo-Savelli had told him?

Troylo-Savelli said, "As I love honor and an honest name, I falter not, my Livio, in one syllable."

He was saying that he was not lying.

Livio said, "This is astonishing news! It is, it is so — bah, I know it."

Was he convinced? It seemed not.

He continued, "Yet Octavio has a kind heart of his own to girls — young, handsome girls. Yes, yes, so he may. It is granted: He would now and then be piddling, and play the wanton, like a fly that dallies about a candle's flame, then scorches its wings, drops down, and creeps away, ha?"

Troylo-Savelli said, "Hardly that, too. To look upon fresh beauties, to discourse in an unblushing merriment of words, to hear them play or sing, to see them dance, to pass the time in pretty amorous questions, and to read a chaste verse of love or prattle riddles, is the height of his temptations."

Livio said, "Send him joy on it! Congratulate him on it!"

Troylo-Savelli said, "His choices of girls are not of the courtly train nor the city's practice, but the country's innocence.

"He prefers such girls as are gentle-born, not low-born; such girls to whom both gaudiness and ape-like fashions are monstrous; such girls as cleanliness and decency prompt to a virtuous envy; such girls as study a knowledge of no danger, but themselves."

Livio said, "Well, I have lived in ignorance: The ancients, who chatted of the golden age, feigned trifles. Had they dreamt this, they would have truthed — believed and affirmed — it to be Heaven. I mean an earthly Heaven — it is not less than an earthly Heaven."

Troylo-Savelli said, "Yet this bachelor-miracle — Octavio — is not free from the epidemical — universal — headache."

Livio asked, "The yellows?"

This society believed that the mixture of four humors in the body determined one's temperament. One humor could be predominant. The four humors are yellow bile, blood, black bile, and phlegm. If yellow bile is predominant, then the person is choleric (bad-tempered). If blood is predominant, then the person is sanguine (optimistic). If black bile is predominant, then the person is melancholic (sad). If phlegm is predominant, then the person is phlegmatic (calm).

A choleric person suffered from an excess of yellow bile. One form of choler was jealousy, which is anger toward someone; for example, it can be anger against someone whom a person thinks will try to steal his loved one.

Troylo-Savelli said, "Octavio suffers from huge jealous fits.

"He allows no one to enter a certain private apartment except me, his page and barber, with a eunuch, and an old female guardian. It is a favor — not commonly given — to you that the license of your visits to your own sister, now and then, is winked at."

Apparently, Castamela, Livio's sister, was now often visiting — maybe even living among — the three Fancies.

Livio asked, "But why are you his agent? His nephew! It is ominous in nature."

The three Fancies lived in Octavio's palace. Troylo-Savelli could be a threat to sleep with one or more of them.

Troylo-Savelli said, "It is not ominous in policy: Being his heir, I may take truce a little with my own fortunes."

Being Octavio's heir, Troylo-Savelli would try not to do anything that would get him disinherited.

Livio said, "Knowing how things stand, too."

He was punning. A "thing" is a penis, and the verb "stand" means to have an erection.

Troylo-Savelli said, "At certain seasons, as the humor takes him, a company of musicians is permitted peaceably to cheer their solitariness, provided they're strangers, not acquainted near the city — but never the same musicians twice, pardon him that. Nor must their stay exceed an hour, or two at the most, as at this wise wedding."

Secco the barber was going to marry Morosa, the old female guardian of the three Fancies.

Troylo-Savelli continued, "His barber is the master to instruct the lasses both in song and dance. The three Fancies are by him trained in both arts."

Livio said, "A caution happily studied."

Octavio was taking good precautions so that the three Fancies would not have sex with men.

Troylo-Savelli said, "Farther to prevent suspicion, he has married his young barber to the old matron. And even farther, Octavio is well pleased that gossips should mutter that he is a mighty man for the game of love because that takes away all suspicion of his impotence in love-making.

"This strict company he calls his Bower of Fancies."

One then-meaning of "company" was "sexual intercourse."

Troylo-Savelli was saying that Octavio wanted everyone to think that he was sleeping with the three Fancies.

A bower is an inner apartment; this was the private apartment in which the three Fancies stayed.

Livio said, "Yes, and properly, since all his recreations are in fancy."

All the sex that Octavio was having with the three Fancies would have to take place in his imagination.

Livio said, "I'm infinitely taken."

The word "taken" meant "pleased," but another meaning of the word is "conned."

He continued, "Sister! By the Virgin Mary, I wish that I had sisters in plenty, Troylo, so I could bestow them all and turn them into Fancies!

"Fancies! Why, it is a pretty name, I think."

Troylo-Savelli said, "Something remains, which in conclusion shortly shall take thee fuller."

The word "take" meant "please," but another meaning is "con."

Music sounded outside the room.

Troylo-Savelli said, "Listen, the wedding-jollity! With a bride-cake, on my life, to grace the nuptials! Perhaps the ladies will turn songsters."

Livio said, "Silence!"

A song was sung outside the room, and then these people entered in a procession with the bride-cake: Secco and Morosa, followed by Castamela; the three Fancies — Floria, Clarella, and Silvia — the attendant Spadone, and the musicians.

Secco said, "This is surpassingly neat and exquisite, I say, fair creatures. These honors to our ceremony are generous and uncommon. My spouse and myself, with our posterity, shall prostitute — devote — our services to your bounties."

He then said to his bride, "Won't we, duckling?"

Morosa said, "Yes, honeysuckle; and do as much for them one day, if things stand right as they should stand."

Her words contained sexual puns. "Do" meant "have sex," "thing" meant "penis," and "stand" meant "have an erection."

She added, "Bill, pigeon, do; thou shall be my cat-a-mountain, and I thy sweet-brier, honey. We'll lead you to kind examples, pretty ones, believe it; and you shall find us one in one, while hearts do last."

A cat-a-mountain is a leopard or panther.

Secco said, "You are my own, always and forever."

Spadone, one of Octavio's attendants, said, perhaps quietly, "Well said, old touchhole."

A touchhole is a hole through which the gunpowder of a cannon was ignited. The cannon could be disabled by hammering a spike into the touchhole.

An erect penis can also be disabled by being repeatedly "hammered" into a hole that can be touched.

Livio said, "All happiness! All joy!"

Troylo-Savelli said, "Lots of children! A fruitful womb!"

Impossible, considering Morosa's age.

Troylo-Savelli continued, "Thou have a blessing, Secco."

Morosa said, "Indeed he has, sir, if you know all, as I conceive you know enough, if not the whole; for you have, I may say, tried me to the quick through and through, and most of my carriage, from time to time."

Troylo-Savelli had, it seems, known her hole, or at least had repeatedly tried to know her hole.

The "quick" is the sensitive part.

Spadone said to himself, "It would wind-break a moil — a mule — or a ringed mare to vie burdens with her."

Mules are incapable of having progeny.

A ringed mare is a mare wearing a ringed piece of equipment that makes it impossible for her to copulate.

According to Spadone, Morosa's burdens would be a man on top of her in the missionary position.

Morosa asked, "What's that you mumble, gelding, hey?"

Spadone replied, "Nothing, indeed, but that you're a bouncing couple well met, and it would be a pity to part you two, even though you hung together in a smoky chimney."

A smoky chimney sends smoke into a room. To stay in a smoky chimney would be unpleasant.

The word "bounce" can mean "talk bigly" or "beat." Morosa was taking no guff from Spadone.

Morosa said, "It would even be a pity, indeed, Spadone. Thou have a foolish loving nature of thine own, and thou wish well to plain dealings, on my conscience."

The word "dealings" can mean a share of something, such as gifts or cards, or in this case, blows.

Spadone said, "I thank your brideship."

He muttered to himself, "I thank your bawdship."

Floria said about Castamela, "Our 'sister' is not merry."

Clarella said, "Sadness cannot become a bridal harmony."

Silvia said, "At a wedding free spirits are required."

Troylo-Savelli said to Castamela, "You should dispense with serious thoughts now, lady."

"Well said, gentlefolks!" Morosa said.

Livio said to his sister, "Come on, Castamela, come on!"

Several people called out, "A dance! A dance!"

Troylo-Savelli said, "By all means, the day is not complete otherwise."

"Indeed, I'll be excused," Castamela said.

"By no means, lady," Troylo-Savelli replied.

"We all are suitors — petitioners — for you to dance," Secco said.

Castamela replied, "With your pardons, spare me for this time; grant me permission to look on as you dance."

Troylo-Savelli said, "Command your pleasures, lady. Whatever you want.

"Everyone take your partner by the hand. Indeed, Spadone must make one in the dance. These merriments are free."

Spadone was an attendant, but he was welcome to enjoy the festivity.

Spadone said, "With all my heart; I'm sure I am not the heaviest and most melancholy in the company. Strike up the music for the honor of the bride and bridegroom."

Music sounded, and many people danced.

Troylo-Savelli said, "So, so, here's art in motion. On all parts, you have bestirred yourself nimbly."

Morosa said to her new husband, "I could dance now, even until I dropped again; but lack of practice denies me the scope of breath or so. Yet, sirrah, my cat-a-mountain, don't I trip — dance — quickly, and with a grace, too, sirrah?"

"You are as light as a feather," Secco replied.

Spadone said, "Surely, you are not without a stick of liquorice in your pocket, indeed. You have, I believe, stout lungs of your own — you swim about so roundly without rubs, aka impediments. It is a tickling sight to be young still."

Sucking on a piece of candy such as liquorice, aka licorice, gave one a boost of energy.

Nitido entered the room and called, "Madam Morosa!"

"Child?" Morosa answered.

Nitido took her aside, saying, "I need to talk to you in secret."

Spadone said, "That earwig scatters the troop now; I'll go near them to make them mad."

An earwig is a pest, or it is someone who worms him- or herself into someone else's life for evil purposes.

Spadone moved closer to Morosa and Nitido.

Livio said, "The private conversation is about my lord, Octavio, upon my life."

Troylo-Savelli said, "Then we must sever."

They had a very good idea about what was going to happen. It involved separating a couple of people from the others.

Morosa said, "Ladies and gentlemen, your ears."

She looked directly at Spadone, telling him non-verbally to move further away because she did not want him to hear what she and Nitido were saying privately.

Spadone muttered to himself, "Oh, it was ever a wanton monkey … he will wriggle into a starting hole so cleanly … if it had been on my wedding-day … I know what I know."

He was thinking that Nitido was trying to wriggle into a starting-hole.

A starting-hole is a place of refuge. One place of refuge in this house was the Bower of Fancies. The word "hole" has an additional bawdy meaning. Spadone may have thought that Nitido was seeking to make Octavio a cuckold by sleeping with one or more of the three Fancies.

Spadone was also thinking that Nitido was seeking to make Secco a cuckold.

Secco asked, "What are you saying, Spadone?"

Spadone said, "Nothing, nothing; I prate sometimes beside the purpose."

He thought, *Whoreson! Lecherous weasel!*

Secco said about Nitido, "Look, look, look, how officious the little knave is! But —"

Spadone thought, *Why, there's the business; butts on one's forehead are but scurvy butts.*

Butts are horns; Spadone was thinking about the horns of a cuckold.

Morosa said, "Spadone, discharge the fiddlers instantly."

Spadone said, "Yes, I know my postures."

"Postures" are positions. He was referring to his position as an attendant and to sexual positions.

He thought, *Oh, monstrous, butts!*

He exited with the musicians.

Morosa said to Secco, "Attend within, sweeting."

She then said, "I beg your pardons, gentlemen.

"Go to your recreations, dear virgins.

"Page, take care."

Nitido said, "My duty, reverend madam."

Troylo-Savelli said, "Livio, away! Sweet beauties —"

Castamela interrupted, "Brother!"

She did not want him to leave her.

Livio replied, "Quickly I shall return."

He thought, *Now for a round — considerable — temptation.*

Almost everyone began to exit in different directions, but Morosa kept Castamela from leaving.

Morosa said to her, "One gentle word in private with your ladyship. I shall not keep you long."

Castamela said, "What means this hubbub of flying in several different directions like this? Who has frightened them? They don't live at devotion or pension here: They are not attendants or boarders. Please, relieve me of distrust."

Morosa said, "May it please your goodness, you'll find him even in every point as honorable as flesh and blood can vouch him to be."

Castamela said, "Ha! Him! Whom? What him?"

Morosa said, "He will not press you beyond his bounds. He will but chat and trifle, and feel your —"

Castamela interrupted, "Guard me! A powerful Genius! Feel!"

A Genius is a supernatural entity such as a guardian angel. Unfortunately, some supernatural entities — such as demons — are evil.

Morosa continued, "— feel your hands to kiss them — your fair, pure, white hands. What strange business is that? These melting twins of ivory, but softer than the down of turtledoves, shall but feed the appetite —"

Was she talking about twin ivory hands or twin ivory breasts?

Castamela interrupted, "A rape upon my ears!"

Morosa continued, "— shall feed the appetite of his poor ravished eye; should he swell higher in his desires, and soar upon ambition of rising in humility by degrees, perhaps he might crave leave to clap —"

A penis can swell and rise.

One meaning of "clap" is to infect with the clap — a venereal disease.

Castamela said, "Foolish woman, in thy grave sinful!"

Morosa continued, "— clap or pat the dimples where Love's tomb stands erected on your cheeks."

Tombs are connected with death, and in this society "to die" sometimes meant "to have an orgasm." Dimples can be likened to vaginas.

Morosa continued, "Pardon those slight exercises, pretty one, for other than those, his lordship is as harmless a weak implement as ever a young lady trembled under."

Young ladies can tremble under a man while in the missionary position.

Castamela said, "Lordship! Help me, my modest anger! This is likely, then, 'religious' matron, some great man's prison, where virgins' honors suffer martyrdom, and you are their tormentor.

"Let's lay down our ruined names to the insulter's mercy! Let's sport and smile on scandal!

"Rare calamity — thou, Morosa, what have thou trapped me in! You named his lordship. Is he some gallant and fiery youth?"

Morosa said, "No, no, indeed, la! He is a very grave and stale — too old for marriage — bachelor, my dainty one.

"There's the conceit: He's none of your hot rovers, who paw you when they first meet you, and so disfigure your dresses and your sets of blush at once.

"He's wise in years, and of a temperate warmth, mighty in means and power, and in everything liberal and generous. He is a wanton in his wishes, but farther than in his wishes he cannot go because he cannot."

Castamela said, "Cannot? Please, speak plainer. I begin to like thee strangely. What do you mean by 'cannot'?"

Morosa said, "You urge me to answer your question timely and to the purpose: He cannot do — the truth is truth. He cannot do anything. As one should say, that's anything."

In other words: He is impotent, and he cannot have sex.

Morosa continued, "I am presenting the case — just presenting the case — if, indeed, he finds you."

In other words: I am giving you information about what *won't* happen if you meet with him.

Disbelieving her, Castamela thought, *My stars, I thank you for being ignorant of what this old-in-mischief can intend!*

Her stars were her astrological stars, which were supposed to foretell the future. If her stars were ignorant of what Morosa seemed to be trying to make happen, that was good evidence that it would not happen.

Castamela asked, "And so we might be merry — bravely merry?"

Morosa said, "You hit it! What else!"

She thought, *Castamela is cunning.*

She then said out loud, "Look, please lend me your hand, indeed."

Castamela said, "Why, please, take it."

Holding Castamela's hand, Morosa said, "You have a delicate and moist palm."

A moist palm was a sign of lechery.

Morosa then said, "Um, can you relish that tickle there?"

She tickled Castamela's hand.

Castamela answered, "And laugh, if there were need to laugh."

Morosa said, "And laugh! Why, now you have it; what hurt, please, do you perceive?"

In other words, perhaps: What hurt is there in engaging in lechery?

She released Castamela's hand.

Morosa continued, "There's all, all. Go on, you need tutoring, but you are an apt scholar. I'll neglect no pains for your instruction."

Castamela said, "Do not."

The word "do" can mean "have sex."

She continued, "But his lordship — who may his lordship be?"

Morosa answered, "No worse a man than Octavio, the Marquis of Siena, the great master of this small family. Your brother has found him to be a bounteous benefactor. Octavio has advanced him and given him the position of the gentleman of the horse. In a short time, Octavio intends to visit you himself in person, as kind and as loving — an old man!"

Castamela said, "We'll meet him with a full flame of welcome. Is it really the Marquis? No worse man than he?"

"A full flame of welcome" could be "a fiery 'welcome.'"

Morosa replied, "No worse, I can assure your ladyship. He is the only free maintainer of the Fancies."

"Fancies!" Castamela said. "What do you mean by that?"

Morosa answered, "The pretty souls who are companions in the house; they are all daughters to honest virtuous and very worshipful and reputable parents — the Fancies are a kind of chaste collapsed ladies."

"Collapsed" means "fallen."

It was easy to get the idea that the Fancies were fallen ladies who lived in a harem: the Bower of the Fancies.

Castamela asked, "Chaste, too, and yet collapsed?"

"Only in their fortunes," Morosa said.

Castamela said, "Surely, I must be a Fancy in the number."

Morosa said, "A principal Fancy. I hope you'll fashion your entertainment, when the Marquis courts you, so that I may stand blameless."

Castamela replied, "Free yourself of that worry.

"Octavio is my brother's raiser? He raised my brother's social status and wealth?"

Morosa said, "Yes, and only Octavio did that."

Castamela asked, "He is my supporter?"

Morosa answered, "Undoubtedly."

Octavio was paying her living expenses.

Castamela asked, "He is an old man — and a lover?"

One kind of love is Platonic love.

Morosa answered, "That is true, and there's the music, the content, the harmony."

Castamela asked, "And I myself am a Fancy?"

Morosa answered, "You are pregnant."

By "pregnant," Morosa meant, "perceptive — full of the right ideas."

Castamela said, "The chance is thrown; I now am fortune's minion; I will be bold and resolute."

The word "chance" can mean 1) opportunity or 2) fate. The die has been thrown, and the result could be a good or a bad fate.

The word "minion" can mean 1) favorite, 2) darling, or 3) lover.

Morosa said, "God's blessing on thee!"

CHAPTER 3
— 3.1 —

Romanello stood alone on a street.

He said to himself, "Prosper me now, my fate! May some better Genius than such a one as waits on troubled passions direct my courses to a noble conclusion!

"My thoughts have wandered in a labyrinth; but if the clue I have laid hold on does fail, I shall tread-out the toil of these dark paths, in spite of politic reaches — shrewd schemes.

"I am punished in my own hopes by the unlucky fortunes of her whose reputation is ruined: Flavia, my lost sister!

"She is lost to reputation because of her unworthy husband, although heightened by a greatness, in whose mixtures I hate to claim a part."

Flavia had been sold by her first husband, the bankrupt merchant Fabricio, to a rich man, Julio de Varana, lord of Camerino, who was now her husband.

Nitido entered the scene.

Romanello said, "Oh, welcome, welcome, dear boy! Thou keep time with my expectations as justly as the promise of my bounties shall reckon with thy service."

Nitido had arrived promptly at the time they had appointed to meet.

Nitido said, "I have arranged the means of your admittance."

"Precious Nitido!" Romanello said.

Nitido added, "More, I have thought of a disguise, a quaint one, that you may appear in and be safe and unsuspected."

"Thou are an ingenious boy," Romanello said.

Nitido added, "Beyond all this, I have so contrived the feat, that at first sight Troylo himself shall court your entertainment, indeed, force you to bestow it."

"Thou have outdone all counsel and all cunning," Romanello said.

Nitido said, "It is true that I have, sir, thrived nimbly in my proceedings, but surely there are some certain hindrances — some roguish staggers, I shall call them — in the business."

Romanello said, "Nitido, what! Faint now! Dear heart, bear up. What staggers? What hindrances? Let me remove them."

Nitido asked, "Am I honest in this discovery?"

He was asking this: Am I doing the right thing?

Romanello replied, "Honest! Bah, is that all?"

He gave him a purse of money.

He continued, "By this rich purse, and by the twenty ducats which are inside it, I will answer for thy honesty against all Italy, and prove thy honesty to be perfect. Besides, remember that I am bound to secrecy — and thou shall not betray thyself."

Nitido said, "All fears are cleared, then. But if —"

Romanello said, "If what? Out with it."

Nitido said, "If we're discovered, you'll say that I am honest always?"

Romanello asked, "Do thou doubt it?"

Nitido replied, "Not much. I have your purse in pawn for it. Now let's talk about the disguise. You know the wit in Florence who in the Great Duke's court burlesques the Duke according to the change of foods in season at every free lord's table."

The wit burlesqued the Duke in accordance with whatever type of humor was fashionable at the time.

Romanello said, "Or free meetings in taverns: there he sits at the upper end, and eats and prates; he doesn't care about how he prates or what he prates about — he is the very quack of fashions, the very man who wears a stiletto-like beard on his chin?"

"You have him — he is the man I mean," Nitido said. "Like such a thing you must appear, and strive, among the ladies, while wearing a formal foppery, to vent some curiosity of language above their apprehensions or your own, indeed beyond sense. The more you do these things, the more you're the person."

Romanello was supposed to wear ostentatious clothing and talk using figures of speech that made little or no sense.

Nitido continued, "You will be now amorous, then scurvy, sometimes bawdy — the same man always, but forevermore fantastic, as being the suppositor to laughter: It has saved expenses in medicine."

A suppositor is a suppository, a medicine. A suppositor can also be a supporter. The wit excites laughter, laughter is the best medicine, and so the wit's audience saves on medicinal costs.

Romanello said, "When opportunity offers itself — for whether it does or not, I will be bold to take it — I may turn to someone in the company, and, changing my method, I will talk of state, and rail against the employment of the time, dislike the behavior of people in important public positions, and dislike that men of parts — of merit — such as I myself am, are not thrust into public action. It will set off a privilege I challenge from opinion with a more lively current."

In other words: When he had the opportunity, he would talk about a somewhat different topic. He would complain about the times and complain that people such as himself were not running society.

This would be an unpopular opinion for many people. He would be complaining about the aristocracy and saying he preferred a meritocracy, with himself as an example of a person of merit. Aristocrats would dislike that opinion, and few people would regard the wit as a person of merit.

Nitido said, "I swear by my modesty that you are some kin to him. Seignior Prugniolo! Seignior Mushrumpo!"

The Italian *prugnolo*, or *prugnolo gentile*, is one of many synonyms of Sangiovese, a grape variety used to make prized wine. In addition, *prugnolo* is the name of an edible mushroom: *Calocybe gambosa*, commonly known as St. George's mushroom.

Figuratively, mushrooms are social upstarts.

Nitido continued, "Just leap into his antic garb, and trust me: You'll fit it to a thought."

Romanello asked, "The time? When?"

Nitido replied, "As quickly as you can be transformed. As for the event, it is pregnant. The time is at hand."

Romanello said, "Yet, my pretty knave, thou have not revealed to me where fair Castamela lives, nor how, nor among whom."

Nitido said, "Bah! Yet more questions? Until your own eyes inform you of the answer, be silent, or else take back your money. What, shall you act like a woman? Bah! Shall you be idle and inquisitive?"

Romanello answered, "No longer. I shall be quickly ready. Ask for a note at my own lodging."

"I'll not fail you," Nitido said.

Romanello exited.

Nitido said to himself, "Assuredly, I will not fail you, Seignior, my fine inamorato — lover! Twenty ducats! They're half his quarter's income.

"Love, oh, love, what a pure madness are thou! I shall fix him. I shall fix, quit, and split him, too."

Troylo-Savelli entered the scene.

Seeing Troylo-Savelli coming toward him, Nitido said, "Most bounteous sir!"

Troylo-Savelli said, "Boy, thou are quick and trusty. Be in everything secret and silent, and thy pains shall meet a liberal reward."

Nitido replied, "Although, sir, I'm only a child, yet you shall find me —"

Troylo-Savelli finished Nitido's sentence, "— a man in the contrivings."

He added, unnecessarily, "I will speak for thee."

He then asked, "Well, does he relish the disguise?"

Nitido answered, "Most greedily. He swallows it with a liquorish delight, and he will immediately assume the disguise — instantly.

"And, I swear on my conscience, sir, the supposition, strengthened by imposition, will transform him into the beast he resembles."

In other words: The suspicion strengthened by the assumption of disguise will transform him into the beast he resembles: the monster of jealousy.

Troylo-Savelli gave him some money and said, "Spend that, and look for more to come, boy."

Nitido said, "Sir, it is not necessary. I have already twenty ducats pursed in a gay case. Alas, sir, to you my service is only my duty."

Nitido was subtly saying that the money that Troylo-Savelli had given to him was very little compared to the money that Romanello had given to him.

Picking up on the sarcasm, Troylo-Savelli said, "'Modesty' in pages is not a virtue, boy, when it exceeds good manners.

"Where must we meet?'

Nitido answered, "Sir, at his lodging, or near there. He will make haste, believe it."

Troylo-Savelli said, "Await the opportunity, and give me notice. I shall attend."

Nitido said, "If I miss my part, hang me!"

Vespucci and Camillo talked together in an apartment in Julio's house. Camillo and Vespucci were Julio's attendants.

Vespucci said, "Come, thou are caught, Camillo."

"Leave! Leave!" Camillo said. "That would be a jest indeed; I caught?"

Vespucci said, "The lady — Floria — scatters glances, wheels around, and smiles. She steals the opportunity to ask what minutes each hour has run in progress.

"Then thou kiss all thy four fingers, crouch, and sigh faintly, 'Dear beauty, if my watch keeps fair decorum and time, three quarters have nearly passed the figure X,' or as the time of day goes."

"So, Vespucci!" Camillo said. "This will not do. I read it on thy forehead, the grain of thy complexion is quite altered. Once it was a comely brown, it is now lately a perfect green and yellow; it surely prognosticates of the overflowing of the gall and melancholy — symptoms of love and jealousy. Poor soul!"

Vespucci was a man, but many young girls of the time suffered from "green-sickness." Falling in love was thought to cause this illness, and having sex was thought to cure it. This is one reason why the color green became associated with unrequited love.

Camillo continued, "Said she, the lady, 'Why do thy locks hang like bell-ropes that are out of their wheels?'"

The locks are locks of hair.

Camillo continued, "Thou, flinging down thy eyes low at her feet, replied, 'Because, oh, sovereign, the great bell of my heart is cracked, and never can ring in tune again until it is newly cast by only one skillful foundress!'"

A foundress is a female worker in a foundry: a place for casting metal, such as bells.

Camillo continued, "At this she turned aside and winked. Thou stood still, and stared. I did see it. Be plainspoken. What hope do I have?"

He was in love — or lust, perhaps — with Flavia, the wife of his employer: Julio de Varana, lord of Camerino.

Vespucci answered, "She loves thee, dotes on thee. In my hearing, she told her lord that Camillo was the Pyramus and Thisbe of courtship and of courtesy."

Pyramus and Thisbe are famous lovers of mythology, but it is odd that Camillo would be compared to both a male lover and a female lover. Such a comment may not be as complimentary as it may sound at first.

Vespucci continued, "Ah, ha! She nicked it there!"

He meant that she had hit the target. In this society, a nick can be a vulva. That is a mark that Camillo no doubt would like to hit with his arrow.

Vespucci continued, "I don't envy thy fortunes, for to say the truth, thou are handsome and deserve her, and you would still deserve her even if she were twice as great as she is now."

As the wife of Julio de Varana, lord of Camerino, Flavia greatly outranked Camillo.

"I handsome?" Camillo said. "Alas, alas, I am a creature of Heaven's making, that's all! But, sirrah, please, let's be sociable and friendly.

"I do confess that I think the good madam may possibly be embraced. I resolve, too, to put in for a share, come what can come of it."

Vespucci said, "A pretty toy it is."

Did he mean Flavia or Camillo?

He continued, "Since thou are open-breasted, Camillo, I will be, too.

"I presume she is wanton, and therefore thou intend to swoop like a bird of prey whenever thou find the game on wing."

Camillo said, "Let us consider that she's only a merchant's leavings."

Vespucci said, "She was hatched in the country, and fledged in the city."

A fledgling is a young bird that has grown and knows how to fly.

Camillo said, "It is a common custom among friends — they are not friends, otherwise — chiefly gallants, to trade by turns in such frail — morally weak — commodities.

"The one is but reversioner — successor — to the other."

Vespucci said, "Why, it is the fashion, man."

Camillo said, "A most free and proper fashion: One surgeon, one apothecary."

He was talking about sharing Flavia with Vespucci, his friend.

Vespucci said, "Do thus, then.

"When I am absent, use the gentlest memory of my endowments, of my unblemished services to ladies' favors, and with what faith and secrecy I live in her commands, whose special courtesies oblige me to particular engagements. I'll do as much for thee."

Camillo said, "With this addition: Tell the best of fairs — the most beautiful woman, Flavia — that Camillo is a man so bashful, so simply harmless, and in addition so constant, yet resolute in all true rights of honor that to deliver him in perfect character would be to detract from such a solid virtue as reigns not in another soul. He is —"

Vespucci finished the sentence for him: "— the thing a mistress ought to wish her servant to be."

In this society, the word "servant" could also mean "lover."

Vespucci then asked, "Are we agreed?"

"Most readily," Camillo said. "On the other side, to the lord her husband let us talk as coarsely of one another as we can."

Vespucci said, "I like it. So shall we sift her love and his opinion."

They had agreed to try to seduce Flavia — and to help each other do so.

Julio, Flavia, and Fabricio entered the room.

Julio said to Fabricio, "Be thankful, fellow, to a noble mistress. Two hundred ducats are no trifling sum nor are they common alms."

He was giving Fabricio two hundred ducats — a lot of money — to go away and not annoy them any more.

Flavia said, "You must not loiter lazily, and speak about the town, my friend, in taverns and in gaming-houses, nor must you sneak after dinner to public shows, to interludes, in riot, to some lewdly painted baggage, tricked-up gaudily like one of us."

She was referring to a non-gentle woman attempting to copy — gaudily — the dress of women above her station in life.

She continued, "Oh, fie upon them, the giblets!"

"Giblets" have little value.

Flavia continued, "I have been told that they ride in coaches, flaunt it in braveries so rich that it's scarcely possible to know how to distinguish one of these vile naughty packs from true and arrant ladies."

"Braveries" are articles of splendid clothing.

A pack is a piece of baggage; baggage is a strumpet.

"Arrant" means "complete" and "genuine," but it usually refers to something that or someone who is completely and genuinely bad, as in "arrant thief."

Flavia had risen from being the wife of a merchant to being the wife of a lord, but she did not like her rise.

She continued, "They'll inveigle your substance and your body, think on that. I say, your body. Look to it: Expect it to be true."

She turned to Julio and asked, "Isn't that sound advice?"

"It is more than sound," Julio said. "It is Heavenly."

Vespucci whispered, "What hope, Camillo, now, do we have if this tune holds?"

The tune was Flavia's speaking out against lecherous women.

Camillo whispered back, "Fair enough hope, Vespucci, now as ever. Why, any woman in her husband's presence can say no less."

Vespucci whispered back, "That's true, and she has freedom here."

Fabricio said to Flavia, "Madam, your care and charity at once have so newly molded my resolves, that henceforth whenever my mention falls into report, it shall requite this bounty. I am travelling to a new world."

In other words: To requite their generosity, he would behave in such a way that whenever he was mentioned, the report of him would be positive.

Julio said, "I like your undertakings."

He wanted Fabricio to go far away.

"New world!" Flavia said. "Where's that, I ask? Good man, if you light on a parrot or a monkey that has the qualities of a new fashion, think about me."

"Yes, lady," Fabricio said. "I, I shall think about you; and my devotions, tendered where they are due in sincere meekness, with purer flames will mount, with liberal increase of plenty, honors, full contents, full blessings, truth and affection between your lord and you."

In this culture, wives called their husbands "lord."

Fabricio continued, "So, with my humblest, best leave, I turn away from you. Never, as now I am, will I appear before you.

"May all joys dwell here, and be lasting!"

Fabricio exited.

Flavia said to Julio, her new husband, "Please, sweetest, listen in your ear."

She leaned toward him, her head hit his hat, and she said, "Curse it, the brim of your hat struck my eye."

Tears flowed down her face.

She thought, *Disguise, honest tears, the griefs my heart labors in. My heart smarts immeasurably.*

Flavia was crying because her first husband was leaving and going far away, not because her eye had hit the brim of her second husband's hat.

Julio held a handkerchief against her face.

Julio said, "An accident! An accident! It will stop — quickly stop. Endure it. This handkerchief is only making it worse."

Camillo advised, "Wink, madam, with that eye. The pain will quickly pass."

"It will pass immediately," Vespucci said. "I know it by experience."

Flavia said, "Yes, I find that the pain is passing."

Julio said, "Leave us for a little time, gentlemen."

Camillo and Vespucci exited.

Julio said to his wife, "Speak freely. What were thou saying, dearest?"

He meant: What were you going to say when you started to whisper in my ear?

Flavia asked, "Do you love me? Answer in sober seriousness. I'm your wife now. I know my place and power."

"What's this riddle?" Julio asked. "Thou have thyself replied to thine own question in being married to me; that is a sure argument of more than protestation."

In other words: Julio's being married to her was a more definite affirmation of his love for her than mere words could be.

Flavia said, "Such it would be, if you were like other husbands. It is granted that a woman of my state may like good clothes, a choice diet, many servants, and change of merriments. All these I do enjoy, and why not? Great ladies should command their own delights.

"And yet, for all this, I am treated but homely, but I am served even well enough."

Flavia had much in the way of material possessions and entertainments, but something was missing. That something was something that she had had with her first husband.

Julio said, "My Flavia, I don't understand what thou want."

Flavia said, "Please pardon me. I confess I'm foolish, very foolish. Trust me, indeed I am foolish, for I could cry my eyes out, being in the weeping mood.

"You know I have a brother."

Julio replied, "Yes, your brother is Romanello, an unkind brother."

Flavia said, "Right, right; since you bosomed my latter youth, he never would agree as much as to come near me. Oh, it maddens me, being but two — only a brother and a sister are left in my family — that we should live at a distance, as if I were a castaway; and you, for your part, do not bother yourself about it, nor do you attempt to draw him here."

Julio said, "Let's admit that the man is peevish. Must I petition him?"

Flavia replied, "Yes, indeed, you must, or else you don't love me.

"Not see my brother!

"Yes, I will see him; so I will. I will see him. You hear it.

"Oh, my good lord — my dear, gentle lord — please. You shall not be angry.

"Alas, I know that the poor gentleman bears a troubled mind, but let him and me meet and talk a little. We perhaps may chide each other at first, shed some few tears, and then be quiet.

"There's all."

Julio said, "Write to him, and invite him here, or go to him thyself. Come, no more sadness; I'll do what thou wish."

Flavia said, "And, in requital, believe that I shall say something that may settle a constancy of peace, for which thou shall thank me."

The constancy of peace could be both between Flavia and her brother, and between Flavia and her husband.

Secco and Spadone spoke together in an apartment in the palace.

Secco said, "He is the most splendid fellow, Spadone! So full of verbal and physical leaps! He talks so humorously, doesn't he? So carelessly! Oh, rich! I swear on my hope of posterity that I could be in love with him."

He was talking about Romanello — who was disguised as the comic wit Prugnuolo.

Spadone said, "His tongue trolls like a mill-clacker. He roughhouses the lady-sisters about as a tumbling dog does young rabbits. Hey, here! Dab, there!"

A "dab" is a slight blow.

He continued, "Your Madonna — that is, your wife, Morosa — he has a catch at her, too. There's a trick in the business, or I am a dunce. I say there is a shrewd trick in the business."

Secco said, "You jump with me to the same conclusion! I smell a trick, too — if I could only tell what it is!"

"Who brought him in?" Spadone said. "Someone would know that."

"Seignior Troylo brought him in," Secco said. "I saw the page, Nitido, depart at the door. Some trick still. Bah! My wife! I must and I will have an eye to this business."

Spadone said, "It's a plain case of roguery — pandering and roguery — or call me a bull calf."

A calf is a fool.

He continued, "Fancies, said he? Rather Frenzies. We shall all roar shortly, turn madcaps, lie open to what comes first. I may stand to it, that boy page is a naughty boy page.

"Let me feel your forehead."

He felt for the cuckold's invisible horns.

Feeling, he said, "Ha! Oh, hmm, yes, there! There again!

"I'm sorry for you, a handsaw cannot cure you. The horns are monstrous and apparent!"

Secco said, "What! What! What! What! What! What do you feel, Spadone?"

Spadone said, "What! What! What! What! Nothing but velvet tips. You are of the first head still."

When a buck first gets its horns, they are covered with soft tissue that is known as velvet.

He continued, "Have a good heart, man. A cuckold, although he may be a beast, wears invisible horns; if he did not, we might not be able to distinguish between a city-bull and a country-calf. Villainous boy, still!"

Bulls have horns, while calves do not. Since a cuckold's horns are invisible, the cuckold is like a calf. In this society, one meaning of the word "calf" is "fool." The horns of a bull, on the other hand, are visible, and bulls are known for potency. Many jokes are told about a city fella taking advantage of a farmer's daughter. Because the cuckolds' horns are invisible, while the city-bulls' horns are visible, we can distinguish between a city-bull and a country-calf. The horns of city-bulls are erect phalluses, which are visible.

The villainous boy was the page Nitido.

"My razor shall be my weapon," Secco the barber said. "Yes, my razor shall be my weapon."

Spadone said, "Why, he's not come to the honor of a beard yet; he needs no shaving."

Nitido was still too young to have a beard.

"I will trim him and tram him," Secco said.

A tram is one of the two upright posts of a gallows. Secco was threatening to cut off Nitido's arms and one leg. Nitido's sin was apparently accepting a bribe to let the newcomer in the palace, where he had an opportunity to make Secco a cuckold.

Spadone said, "Nay, she may do well enough for one."

For one lover.

"For one!" Secco said. "Ten, a hundred, a thousand, ten thousand; do beyond arithmetic!"

The word "do" means "have sex."

He continued, "Spadone, I speak it with some passion: I am a notorious cuckold."

It took very little for him to be convinced of that.

"Gross and ridiculous!" Spadone said. "Look. I tell you point-blank that I dare not swear that this same mountebanking newly come foist is at least a procurer in the business, if not a pretender himself; but I think what I think."

A mountebank is a conman. A foist is a rogue. A pretender is a wooer.

Secco said, "The newcomer, Troylo, Livio, and the page, that hole-creeping page, all put horns on my forehead, sirrah."

A hole-creeping page is a page who creeps into holes.

Secco continued, "I'll forgive thee from my heart if you answer this: Don't thou drive a trade, too, in my bottom?"

A bottom is a deep place.

Secco was asking if Spadone was prostituting Morosa.

Spadone deflected the question by pretending that Secco was asking if he, Spadone, was sleeping with his wife: "A likely matter! Alas, I'm metamorphosed, I am."

Spadone was thought to be a eunuch: That was his metamorphosis.

He continued, "Be patient, or you'll mar everything."

They heard laughing coming from another room: "Ha, ha, ha, ha!"

Secco said, "Now, now, now, now the game's rampant — rampant!"

Spadone said, "Leave your wild figaries — whims — and learn to be a meek grotesque, or I'll observe no longer."

Secco was a grotesque because of the invisible horns he believed that he was wearing.

The laughter continued: "Ha, ha, ha, ha!"

Troylo-Savelli, Castamela, Morosa, and Romanello — who was disguised as Prugnuolo — entered the room. With them were the three Fancies: Floria, Clarella, and Silvia. Castamela may have believed — or known — that others regarded her as soon becoming the fourth Fancy.

Silvia said to the disguised Romanello, "You are extremely busy, Seignior."

Floria said, "You are courtly, without a fellow."

Clarella said, "You have a stabbing wit."

Castamela said, "But are you always, when you press on ladies of mild and easy nature, so much of a satirist, so tart and keen as we do taste you now? It argues a lean brain."

A lean brain lacks some qualities that others consider important. Castamela was most likely thinking of decorum.

The disguised Romanello said, "Bah to your beauties! You would be fair — truly, you would be monsters. Fair women are such. Monsters are rare to be seen, and so are fair women."

Troylo-Savelli said, "Bear with him, ladies. Endure what he says."

"He is a foul-mouthed man," Morosa said.

Secco whispered to Morosa, "Whore, bitch-fox, treddle! Fa la la la!"

A treddle is a pellet of sheep manure.

"What's that, my cat-a-mountain?" Morosa asked. "What did you say to me?"

Spadone said to Secco, "Hold her there, boy."

Secco, Morosa, and Spadone formed one group. The three Fancies, Castamela, Troylo-Savelli, and the disguised Romanello formed another.

Clarella asked the disguised Romanello, "Were you ever in love, fine Seignior?"

The disguised Romanello replied, "Yes, for sport's sake, but I soon forgot it; he who rides at a gallop is quickly weary. I esteem love as I esteem a man in some huge place; it puzzles reason, distracts the freedom of the soul, renders a wise man a fool, and a fool a wise man in his own imagination, but nowhere else. It makes the effects of pleasure into those of travail; the effects of bitter into those of sweet; the effects of war into those of peace; the effects of thorns into those of roses; the effects of prayers into those of curses; the effects of longings into those of surfeits — and then there is despair, and then a rope.

"Oh, my fine lover!

"Yes, I have loved a score at once."

In the other group, Spadone said to Secco, "Bah, stallion! As I am a man and no man, the baboon lies, I dare swear, abominably."

The baboon was Morosa, who apparently had said bad things about Spadone.

Secco said about Morosa's supposed lying, "Inhumanly."

He then said to her, "Keep your bow close, vixen."

A bow forms part of a circle. Secco was telling his wife to keep her circle — her vagina — close, aka hidden. In other words: He was telling her to be chaste.

Secco pinched his wife, Morosa.

She said to him, "Curse your fingers, if you are in earnest and not joking! You pinch too hard! Bah! I'll pare your fingernails because you are pinching me."

Spadone said to Secco, "She means she will pare your horns; there's a bob — a cut — for you!"

In the other group, Clarella said to the disguised Romanello, "Spruce Seignior, if a man may love so many, why mayn't a fair lady have the like privilege of several servants?"

The word "spruce" meant "dapper." The servants were wooers.

Troylo-Savelli said, "Answer that: The reason holds the same weight."

In other words: What's good for the gander — a male goose — is good for the female goose.

In the other group, Morosa said, "Indeed, and so it does, although he would spit his gall out."

She meant that her bow was close and she was chaste, although her husband was angry at her and spitting out gall in the form of angry words.

Spadone said, "Remember that, Secco."

In the other group, Silvia asked the disguised Romanello, "Do you struggle for a reply?"

He had not answered Clarella's question immediately.

The disguised Romanello said, "The learned differ in that point; grand and famous scholars often have argued pro and con, and left the answer doubtful. Volumes have been written on it. If, then, great clerks suspend their resolutions, it is modest for me to silence mine. If great scholars cannot answer the question, then I ought to be quiet."

"That answer is dull and phlegmatic — it's sluggish!" Floria said.

Clarella said, "Yet women, surely, in such a case are always more secret than men are."

"Yes," Silvia said, "and they talk less."

The disguised Romanello said, "That is a 'truth' much fabled, but never found. You women secret!

"When your dresses blab your vanities?

"You use the color of carnations for your laces? There's a woman who is a gross babbler!

"Wear tawny — the color brown? Ha! The pretty woman's heart is wounded.

"Does she wear a knot of willow-ribbons? She's forsaken."

The willow is a symbol of unrequited love.

The disguised Romanello's point was that what women wore revealed their state of mind.

"Another rides the cock-horse — she is high-spirited — and wears green and azure — she kicks and cries 'wee-hee!' like an unbroken colt."

A cock-horse is either a child's plaything that the child can pretend to ride like a horse, or it is a high-spirited horse.

He continued, "But desperate black puts women in mind of fish-days, days during which no meat is served — when Lent spurs on devotion, there's a famine.

"Yet love and judgment may help all this pudder — this fuss.

"Where are they? Where are love and judgment? Not in females."

Floria said, "In all sorts of men, no doubt."

Silvia said, "Else they were sots to choose —"

Sots are fools.

Silvia probably meant to finish her sentence with something such as "a woman to love."

Clarella interrupted and finished Silvia's sentence: "— to swear and flatter, and sometimes lie, for profit."

The profit could be to get a woman in bed.

The disguised Romanello said, "That is not so, truly: Should love and judgment meet each other, then the old, the foolish, the ugly, and the deformed could never be beloved."

If love and judgment met in each of us, wouldn't we all fall in love with someone young rather than with someone old? With someone smart rather than foolish? With someone good-looking rather than ugly? With someone healthy rather than deformed?

The disguised Romanello continued, "For example, look at these two: this madam and this shaver."

A shaver can be 1) a barber, 2) a swindler, and/or 3) a wag.

The disguised Romanello was referring to the aged female guardian Morosa and her husband Secco, the barber.

Insulted, Morosa said, "I defy thee! Am I old or ugly?"

Secco said, "Tricks, deceits, devices! Now it trolls — wags — about."

A tongue wags — Secco meant: Now it comes out verbally.

The disguised Romanello said, "Truly let it go, young stripling. Thou have still firm footing, and thou need not fear the cuckold's livery — horns.

"There's good reason for it. Take this for comfort. No horned beasts have teeth in either gums, but thou are toothed on both sides, though she fail in having teeth."

Most people would say that horned beasts such as cows do have teeth in their gums; however, the word "gums" is also used to refer to toothless gums, so the disguised Romanello, a wag whose words don't always make normal sense, was saying this: "No horned beasts have teeth in either toothless gums."

The disguised Romanello was also saying that Secco had teeth on both sides: top and bottom. Again, this is not the way we normally use language.

If the disguised Romanello was wrong about "No horned beasts have teeth in either gums" and "thou are toothed on both sides" and perhaps "though she fail in having teeth" (since Morosa insisted that she has teeth, then perhaps he was wrong in saying about Secco that "thou need not fear the cuckold's livery — horns."

Morosa said, "My husband is not jealous, sirrah."

The disguised Romanello said, "That's his fortune. Women, indeed, are more jealous than men, but men have more cause."

Spadone said, "There he rubbed your forehead; it was a tough blow."

Spadone was twisting the disguised Romanello's words: Earlier, the disguised Romanello had said that Secco did not need to fear horns.

"It smarts," Secco said.

"A pox on him!" Morosa said about the disguised Romanello. "Let him put his finger into any gums of mine, he shall find I have teeth about me — sound ones!"

Secco said to the disguised Romanello, "You are a scurvy fellow, and I am made a cokes, an ass —"

A "cokes" is a fool.

He continued, "— and this same filthy crone's a flirt."

He then recited the refrain of a popular song: "*Whoop, do me no harm, good woman.*"

Secco exited.

Spadone said, "Now, now he's in! I must not leave him so."

Spadone had been trying — and succeeding — in making Secco think that his wife, Morosa, was cuckolding him.

Spadone exited.

Troylo-Savelli asked, "Morosa, what is the meaning of this?"

"I don't know," Morosa replied. "He pinched me, and he called me names — very filthy names."

She then said to the disguised Romanello, "Will you depart from here, sir? I will set you packing."

She exited.

Clarella said to the disguised Romanello, "You were, indeed, too outspoken, too violent."

"Here nothing was meant but mirth," Floria said.

"The gentleman has been a little jocular," Silvia said.

"He was somewhat bitter against our sex," Clarella said.

"For which I promise him that he will never prove to be a choice of mine," Castamela said.

The disguised Romanello asked, "I won't be your choice?"

"So she protested, Seignior," Troylo-Savelli said.

Of course, Troylo-Savelli knew who Romanello was, despite his disguise.

The disguised Romanello said, "Indeed!"

Clarella said, "Why, you are moved, sir."

He was deeply affected by what Castamela had said about him.

Morosa re-entered the room.

Morosa said to the disguised Romanello, "Go away from here! There will enter a more civil companion for fair ladies than such a slovenly person as you."

The disguised Romanello began, "Beauties —"

Troylo-Savelli interrupted: "Time prevents us from staying. May love and sweet thoughts accompany this presence."

Troylo-Savelli and the disguised Romanello exited.

Octavio, Secco, and Livio entered the room. Secco was whispering to Octavio.

Octavio said to Secco, "Enough. Slip away, and on your life be secret."

Secco exited.

Octavio then said to the ladies, "A lovely day, young creatures!

"To you, Floria, and to you, Clarella and Silvia, and to all, I am at your service!"

Seeing Castamela, he asked, "But who is this fair stranger?"

Livio said, "This is Castamela, my sister, noble lord."

Octavio said to Castamela, "Let my ignorance of who you were plead my neglect of manners, and let this soft touch excuse it."

He touched her arm and continued, "You've enriched this little family, most excellent virgin, with the honor of your company."

Castamela replied, "I find them worthily graceful, sir."

Livio thought, *Are you so taken with him?*

He did not want his sister to be attracted to Octavio, especially in any improper way.

Octavio said, "Here are no public sights nor courtly visitants, which youth and active blood might stray in thought for. The people are few, and the pleasures are simple and rarely to be enjoyed, perhaps, by any not perfectly acquainted with this custom. Aren't they, lovely one?"

Livio said, "Sir, I dare answer for my sister and give her settled opinion. She has always preferred free conversation among so many of her so-virtuous sex, before the arrogance of solemn promises or the vainer giddiness of popular attendants."

Suitors would be the ones making those solemn promises.

Castamela thought, *Well played, brother!*

Music sounded from another room.

Octavio asked, "What is the meaning of this music?"

Morosa answered, "If it pleases your lordship, it is the ladies' hour for exercise in song and dance."

Octavio said, "I dare not be the author of truanting the time then, and therefore I will not."

"Walk on, dear ladies," Morosa said.

"It is a task of pleasure," Octavio said.

Livio, who could guess what was coming, whispered to Castamela, "Be now my sister, and withstand a trial bravely."

Morosa whispered to Castamela, "Remember my instructions, or —"

She exited, followed by Livio, Floria, Clarella, and Silvia.

Castamela attempted to exit, but Octavio stopped her.

Octavio said, "Begging your pardon, you are not of the number, I presume, yet, to be enjoined to hours. You are not yet one of those studying music and dance here.

"If you please, we for a little while may sit as judges of their proficiency; please, grant the favor."

They could stay in this room and hear the songs the others sang.

Castamela said, "I am, sir, in a place to be commanded, as now the present urges."

She was his guest.

Octavio said, "There is no compulsion. 'Compulsion' would be too hard a word. Where you are sovereign, your yea and nay is law. I have a request to ask of you."

He was not acting like a sovereign: He was requesting, not demanding. Still, many sovereigns who make "requests" are actually making demands.

Castamela asked, "A request for what, sir?"

"For your love," Octavio answered.

Castamela said, "Love to whom? I am not so weary of the authority I hold over my own contentment in sleeps and wakings that I'd resign my liberty to any who would control it."

She was happy being single and having more freedom than she would if she were married.

Octavio said, "I do not intend that. Grant me a request."

"Of what nature?" Castamela asked.

"To acknowledge me your creature," Octavio answered.

If he were her creature, he would be subservient to her in some way. He could be a man who loved her and regarded her more highly than he regarded himself.

Castamela said, "Oh, my lord, you are too wise in years, too full of counsel, for my green inexperience."

Octavio said, "Love, dear maiden, is only desire of beauty, and it is proper for beauty to desire to be beloved.

"I am not free from passion, although the current of a more lively heat runs slowly through me. My heart is gentle; and, believe me, fresh and unsullied girl, thou shall not wish for any good additional thing that may adorn thy excellent qualities to praise them, which bounty can withhold."

Even bounty — generosity — can withhold some things, but even those things would not be withheld from Castamela.

But perhaps "which bounty can withhold" modified "them," aka thy excellent qualities." In that case, "bounty" meant goodness. Castamela's goodness could lead her to withhold some of her excellent qualities, such as virginity, from Octavio.

The word "withhold" can be ambiguous. The *Oxford English Dictionary* gives these meanings, among others: 1) "to keep back," 2) "to keep in bondage," and 3) "to retain for one's pleasure or profit."

Castamela believed that Octavio was offering her his bounty — generosity — in order to keep her in a form of bondage.

Octavio continued, "This academy of silent pleasures is maintained, but only to such a faithful use."

The academy of silent pleasures was Octavio's heart.

Castamela said, "You have, perhaps, then, a patent for concealing virgins; otherwise, make plainer your intentions."

Octavio said, "To be pleasant in practice of some outward senses only. No more."

He was saying that he wanted to share a Platonic love with her.

She did not believe him.

Castamela said, "No worse you dare not to imagine, where such a profound innocence as mine is outfaces every wickedness your dotage has lulled you in. I scent your cruel 'mercies.' Your female agent, your old temptation, your she-devil has been scheming for my misery."

She meant that Morosa had been attempting to persuade her to become one of Octavio's Fancies — one of those women with whom Castamela presumed he had been sleeping.

She apologized for her language: "Bear with a language that this place, and none but this, has infected my tongue with."

She then complained about her brother: "The time will come, too, when he — unhappy man! — whom your advancement has ruined by making him a spaniel to your fortunes, will curse that he enticed me hither: Livio."

A "spaniel" is a person who fawns on his master the way that a cocker spaniel fawns on its master.

Castamela continued talking about Livio: "I must not call him my brother; this one act has torn him from the ancestry he has sprung from."

Octavio said, "The offer of a noble courtesy — a courteous invitation — is checked, it seems. You have declined my offer."

Castamela said, "A courtesy! It is a bondage! You are a great man, vicious, much more vicious because you hold a seeming league with charity. You are of a pestilent nature. You keep hospitality for sensualists in your own sepulcher, even during your lifetime, yet you are dead already."

Octavio said, "What's this? Come, be milder."

Castamela replied, "You chide me soberly. So, then, sir, I tune my voice to other music."

She then listed some of the advantages he possessed and made some recommendations about some virtuous ways to treat the three Fancies:

"You are an eminent statesman.

"Be like a father to such unfriended virgins as your bounty has drawn into a scandal.

"You are powerful in means.

"You are a bachelor, freed from the jealousies of wants.

"Convert this privacy of maintenance into your own court.

"Let this, as you call it, your academy, have a residence there, and there survey your charity yourself.

"Do this so that when you shall bestow the three Fancies on worthy husbands, with fitting portions, such as you know worthy, you may yield to the present age a model of 'virtue' and to posterity a glorious chronicle. There would be a work of piety."

She was saying that he could eventually marry the three Fancies to good husbands, who could provide for them. That would be an act of virtue that he would be known for.

Then she mentioned what she believed his current conduct would lead to:

"The other course of action is a scorn upon your tombstone; where the reader will but expound that when you lived you pandered your own purse and your fame."

She was accusing him of another action: sleeping with the three Fancies. This was something that would be known after his death.

Castamela continued, "I am too bold, sir. Some anger and some pity have directed a wandering trouble."

Octavio said, "Be not known what passages the time has lent."

Perhaps he meant this: Keep this conversation secret.

Or perhaps he meant this: The actions I have done are not known.

He added, "For once I can bear with you."

In other words: On this one occasion, I can bear what you have said to me.

Castamela said, "I'll countenance the hazard of suspicion, and be your guest awhile."

In other words: I will risk being suspected of being one of your Fancies, and I will remain as your guest for a while.

Octavio said, "Be my guest for a while, but thereafter I don't know what."

He called, "Livio!"

Livio and Morosa re-entered the room.

"My lord?" Livio asked.

Castamela said, "Indeed, sir, I cannot part with you yet."

Was she talking to Livio or to Octavio?

If she were talking to Livio, Morosa would perhaps think that Castamela was remaining virtuous.

If she were talking to Octavio, Morosa would perhaps think that Castamela was not remaining virtuous.

Octavio said, "Well, then, thou shall not, my precious Castamela."

Did he know to whom Castamela was speaking?

He then said, "Thou have a sister, a perfect sister, Livio."

Morosa thought, *All is nicked here. Good soul, indeed!*

Perhaps she meant: Castamela has denied Octavio. She is a good soul, indeed!

The verb "nick" can mean "hit the mark." Perhaps Morosa meant that everything was going well; after all, Livio's having a perfect sister is good.

However, the noun "nick" can mean "vulva." If Octavio's "arrow" were to hit Castamella's nick, then Morosa may not consider her to be a good soul.

Telling another person's thoughts is difficult; one can be mistaken.

Perhaps Morosa thought, *All is inked here. "Good" soul, indeed!*

In this case, perhaps she meant: Castamela has not denied Octavio. All is marked with black sin. She is a "good" soul, indeed!

However: although the verb "ink" means "stain," a stain need not be a bad thing. Stained wood can look good. Perhaps, again, Morosa meant that everything was going well.

Livio said, "I'd speak with you soon."

Castamela replied, "It may be so."

Octavio said to Castamela, "Come, fair one."

Livio said to himself, "Oh, I'm cheated!"

He believed that his sister had given in to Octavio and would become his concubine: a fourth Fancy.

CHAPTER 4

— 4.1 —

Livio and Castamela spoke together in an apartment in the palace. Castamela believed that her brother had sold her to Octavio in return for a good job and material prosperity.

Livio said, "Please, be serious."

Castamela replied, "Please, don't interrupt the paradise of my becharming thoughts, which mount my knowledge to the sphere I move in, above this useless tattle."

She was deliberately tormenting her brother by making him believe that she had fallen for Octavio and would or had become one of his Fancies. She wanted her brother to think that she was no longer chaste; he would feel guilty because he had brought her to Octavio's palace.

"Tattle, sister!" Livio said. "Do you know to whom you are saying this?"

Castamela replied, "To the gentleman of my lord's horse, newly stepped into the office! It is a good position, sir, if you can be thankful. Bear yourself with humility in it, so that negligence, or pride of your preferment, will not overpower the grace you hold in Octavio's esteem. Such fortunes do not drop down every day. Respect the favor that raised you to this fortune."

Livio said, "Thou are mistaken, surely, about which person thou are speaking with."

Castamela said, "I am talking to a strange and idle person."

Livio said, "Is it possible? Why, you are turned a mistress, a mistress of the trim."

According to Livio, Castamela had become a very well-dressed, but haughty and proud lady.

Livio also was afraid that she had become one of Octavio's Fancies.

He continued, "Curse me, lady, you keep a stately deportment, but it does not become you.

"Our father's daughter, if I am not greatly mistaken, delighted in a softer, humbler sweetness, not in a hey-de-gay of scurvy gallantry.

"You do not carry it off like a thing of the fashion. You ape the humor faintly."

She was not born to act this way.

Castamela quoted Octavio: "Love, dear maiden, is only desire of beauty, and it is proper for beauty to desire to be beloved."

"This is fine entertainment!" Livio said sarcastically. "You will not mind me; will you yet hear me, madam?"

Castamela again quoted Octavio: "Thou shall not wish for any good additional thing that may adorn thy excellent qualities to praise them, which bounty can withhold."

She then added, "I know I shall not."

Livio said, "And so you applauded and accepted the bargain! The idea of it tickles your contemplation! It has come out now: A woman's tongue, I see, at some time or another, will prove her traitor."

Livio's last words were ambiguous and could mean that a woman's tongue 1) will prove to be a traitor to her, or 2) will prove that she is a traitor.

He continued, "This was all I sifted, and here I have found thee wretched."

He had made trial of her, and he had metaphorically sifted her to separate the fine parts from the coarse parts, but all he had found was wretched.

Castamela said, "We shall flourish. We shall feed high on the hog from henceforth, man, and no more shall we be straitened within the limits of an empty patience, nor will we tire our feeble eyes with only gazing on greatness, which enjoys the sway of pleasures.

"Instead, we ourselves shall be the objects of the envy of those to whom a service would have seemed ambition."

The service — job position — might be being the chief provisor of Octavio's horse.

Castamela continued, "It was thy cunning, Livio; I applaud it.

"Fear nothing; I'll be successful in thy projects.

"Lack? Misery? May all such lack as think about it! Our footing shall stand firm."

She was pretending to rejoice at trading her chastity for the material prosperity of her brother and herself.

Livio said, "You are very witty. Why, Castamela, are you doing this to me? You are very obviously putting on a counterfeit act. I am too well acquainted with thy condition, sister.

"If the Marquis has uttered one unchaste, one wanton syllable, provoking thy contempt, not all the flatteries of his assurance to our hopes of rising in society can, or shall, enslave our souls."

Castamela said, "Indeed, that is not the case, sir. You are beside the point, most gentle Seignior!

"I'll be no more your ward, no longer chambered nor mewed-up and confined to the chain of your devotion.

"Trust me, I must not, will not, dare not. Surely I cannot, for my promise has been passed; and the suffering of former trials has too strongly armed me.

"You may take this for my answer."

She was saying that she was quite happy to be nice to Octavio in return for advancement in society for herself and for her brother, Livio.

Livio said, "Are you in such earnest! Has goodness quite left thee? Fool, thou are wandering in dangerous fogs, which will corrupt the purity of every noble virtue that has dwelt within thee.

"Come home again, home, Castamela, sister, home to thine own innocence; and rather than yield thy reputation up to the witchcraft of an abused confidence and trust, be courted by Romanello."

Castamela said, "Romanello!"

Livio asked, "Do thou scorn the name? Thy thoughts, I find, then, are changed; they are rebels to all that's honest, rebels to all that's truth and honor."

Castamela said, "So they have changed, sir, and in good time!"

Livio said, "Thou have fallen suddenly into a pleurisy — an excess — of faithless impudence. A whorish itch — a leprosy of raging lust — infects thy blood, and thou are mad to prostitute the glory of thy virgin-dowry basely for common sale.

"This foulness must be purged, or thy disease will rankle and grow into a pestilence that can even taint the very air around thee.

"But I shall study and find the medicine that can cure thee."

Castamela replied, "Learn good manners. I take it that you are saucy."

"Saucy!" Livio said. "You are a strumpet in thy desires! It is in my power to cut off the twist thy life is spun by."

He was angry enough to say that he could kill her. In mythology, the three Fates spun the thread of life, measured it, and then cut it when it was time for a person to die.

Castamela said, "Phew! You rave now. But if you have not destroyed all your reason, know that I will use my freedom.

"You, truly and indeed, for a change of fresh apparel, and the pocketing of some well-looking ducats, were contented, surpassingly pleased — yes, by the Virgin Mary, you were; recognize it — to expose me to the danger now you rail at!

"You brought me, nay, forced me hither, without having a question of what might follow.

"Here you find the result, and I don't distrust that it was the appointment of some succeeding fate that more concerned me than widowed virginity."

According to Castamela, her brother preferred that she become a concubine than live to old age as a virgin as long as he gained materially from it.

Livio said, "You're a gallant; you are one of my old lord's Fancies. Peevish, foolish girl, was it ever heard that youth could dote on sickness, a gray beard, a wrinkled face, a dried-up marrow, a toothless head, a — but this is only a merriment, merely only a trial.

"Romanello loves thee. He hasn't abundance and wealth, that is true, yet he cannot be in needy poverty."

Apparently, he had friends who would help him. Or Livio wanted to believe that Romanello had friends who would help him.

Livio added, "Return with me, and I will leave these fortunes, good maiden, of gentle nature."

He was willing to give up his position and higher social standing in order to protect his sister and her reputation.

Castamela continued to plague him: "By my hopes, I never placed affection on that gentleman, although he deserved well. I have told him often my resolution."

She was claiming never to have liked Romanello, at least enough to marry him.

Livio asked, "Will you go away from here, and trust to my care of settling you a peace?"

He would arrange a marriage for her.

Castamela said, "No, surely. Such treaty may break off."

Livio said, "Then off be it broken! I'll do what thou shall rue."

"You cannot, Livio," Castamela said.

"You are so confident!" Livio said. "Young mistress of mine, I'll do it."

Livio exited.

Troylo-Savelli entered the room.

Troylo-Savelli said, "Incomparable maiden!"

Castamela said, "You have been counselor to a strange dialogue."

She either knew or could guess that Troylo-Savelli had overheard the conversation between her and her brother. Since a counselor is an advisor, he may even have advised her on what to say to her brother.

Troylo-Savelli said, "If there is constancy in professing a virtuous nature, you are secure, as the effects — the results — shall witness."

She had professed to Octavio that she had a virtuous nature. To her brother, she had pretended not to have a virtuous nature.

Castamela replied, "Be noble; I am credulous and wanting to believe you.

"My language has prejudiced my heart; I and my brother have never parted at such distance, yet I glory in the fair race he runs. But I fear the violence of his disorder."

She was happy that her brother was so desirous of protecting her reputation, but she was afraid of what his anger might make him do.

Troylo-Savelli said, "A little time shall quit him."

The word "quit" can mean "set free."

According to Troylo-Savelli, a little time would free Livio from his anger.

Hearing some others coming, they retired to a corner where they were somewhat hidden.

Secco entered the room. He had tied a garter to Nitido's neck and was leading him with it in one hand; he had a rod — a whip — in the other.

Following them were Morosa and the three Fancies: Silvia, Floria, and Clarella.

Following them was Spadone, who was laughing.

Secco said, "The young whelp is mad; I must slice the worm out of his breech. I have noosed his neck in the collar; and I will at once turn dog-doctor."

The "worm" was a small ligament in a dog's throat. People in this society believed that cutting it would prevent rabies.

The word "breech" can refer to the loins. In that case, the "worm" would be a piece of male anatomy.

Secco continued, "Stand back from me, or you'll find me terrible and furious."

Nitido begged, "Ladies, good ladies, dear Madam Morosa!"

"Honest Secco!" Floria said.

"What was the cause of this?" Silvia asked. "What wrong has he done to thee?"

Clarella asked, "Why do thou frighten us so, and why are thou so peremptory where we are present, fellow?"

Morosa said, "Honey-bird, spouse, cat-a-mountain! Ah, the child, the pretty poor child, the sweet-faced child!"

Spadone said, "That very word halters the earwig — the parasite."

Morosa's referring to Nitido using kind epithets would only make Secco angry: Secco thought that Nitido had been cuckolding him.

Secco said, "Leave, I say, or I shall lay bare all the naked truth to your faces; his fore-parts have been too lusty, and his posteriors must do penance for it."

He was going to whip Nitido's buttocks.

Secco ordered Nitido, "Untruss, whiskin, untruss!"

He was going to whip Nitido's bare buttocks.

A whiskin is a pander.

Secco ordered, "Leave, burrs!"

He said to his wife, "Leave, mare-hag moil! Avaunt! Leave! Thy turn comes next. Avaunt! The horns of my rage are advanced; go away from here, or I shall gore you!"

Spadone advised, "Lash him soundly; let the little ape show his tricks now."

Nitido begged, "Help, or I shall be throttled!"

Morosa said to him, "Yes, I will help thee, pretty heart; if my tongue cannot prevail, my fingernails shall."

She then said to her husband, Secco, "Barbarous-minded man, let him go, or I shall use my talons."

Morosa and Secco fought.

Spadone said, "Well played, dog! Well played, bear! Sa! Sa! Sa! Go at it! Go at it!"

"Sa!" was a hunting cry that hunters used to encourage their dogs.

Secco yelled, "Fury, whore, bawd, my wife and the devil!"

Morosa yelled, "Toss-pot, stinkard, pander, my husband and a rascal!"

Spadone sang:

"Scold, coxcomb, baggage, cuckold!

"Crabbed age and youth

"Cannot jump together;

"One is like good luck,

"The other is like foul weather."

Troylo-Savelli said to Castamela, "Let us fall in with them now."

He stepped forward with Castamela.

He said, "What uncivil rudeness dares offer a disturbance to this company? Peace and delights dwell here, not brawls and outrage."

He then said to Secco, "Sirrah, be sure you show some reasons why you so forget your duty; quickly show it, or I shall tame your choler: What's the reason for your anger?"

Suddenly becoming aware of Troylo-Savelli's presence, Spadone said to himself, "Hmm, what's that? What's that? Is he there, with a vengeance? I then begin to dwindle."

He needed to take care to stay out of trouble.

He thought of the refrain of an old song:

Oh, oh, the fit, the fit;

The fit's upon me

Now, now, now, now.

Secco said, "The reason for my anger shall be revealed. First, then, all Christian people, Jews and infidels, he's and she's, know by these presents that I am a beast; see what I say, I say a very beast."

He was saying that he was a horned beast: a cuckold.

Troylo-Savelli said, "It is granted: You are a beast."

Secco said, "Go to it, then. I am a horned beast, a goodly tall horned beast; in pure verity, a cuckold. Nay, I will tickle their trangdidos — beat their backsides."

Morosa said, "Ah, thou base fellow! I wish that thou would confess it if it were true that thou are a cuckold, but it is not true. Thou lie, and thou lie loudly."

Troylo-Savelli said, "Have patience, Morosa."

He then said to Secco, "You are, you say, a cuckold?"

Secco replied, "I'll justify my words — I scorn to eat them: This sucking ferret has been wriggling in my old cony-burrow."

A cony-burrow is a rabbit-hole, but it is also slang for a vagina.

He was accusing Nitido of sleeping with his wife, Morosa.

Morosa said to her husband, "The boy, the babe, the infant! I spit at thee."

Castamela said, "Bah, Secco, bah!"

Secco said, "Appear, Spadone! My proofs are pregnant and grossly obvious; truth is the truth; I must and I will be divorced. Speak, Spadone, and exalt thy voice."

"Who? I speak?" Spadone said. "Alas, I cannot speak, I."

Nitido began speaking, "As I hope to live to be a man —"

Secco interrupted, "Damn the prick of thy weason-pipe!"

The prick of Nitido's weason-pipe was the tongue of his throat.

Secco continued, "Where only two lie in a bed, you must be bodkin, bitch-baby, must you?"

A bodkin is a third person wedged into a space where there is room for only two people; in this case, the space is Secco and Morosa's bed.

Secco asked, "Spadone, am I a cuckold or not a cuckold?"

Spadone was the person who had been misleading Secco into believing that he was a cuckold. As would become clear later, Spadone was doing this to get revenge on Nitido for teasing him about being a eunuch.

Spadone said, "Why, you know I am an ignorant, unable trifle in such business, an oaf, a simple alcatote, an innocent."

An alcatote is a silly person.

Secco said, "Nay, nay, nay, that doesn't matter; this ramkin — young ram — has tupped my old rotten carrion-mutton. Nitido has had sex with my wife, Morosa."

Insulted at being called an old rotten carrion-mutton, Morosa said to Secco, "You are rotten in thy mouth, thy guts, and thy garbage!"

In this context, "garbage" meant an animal's entrails.

Secco said, "Spadone, speak aloud what I am."

"I do not know," Spadone replied.

Secco asked, "What have thou seen them doing together, doing?"

The word "do" can mean "have sex."

"Nothing," Spadone said.

Morosa asked Secco, "Are thy mad brains in thy head now, thou jealous bedlam — thou lunatic?"

Secco asked Spadone, "Didn't thou, from time to time, tell me as much?"

"Never," Spadone replied.

Secco said, "Hoy-day! Ladies and Seignior, I am being abused. They have agreed to scorn, jeer, and run me out of my wits, with their voluntary consent. This gelded hobet-a-hoy is a corrupted pander, the page a milk-livered dildo, my wife a confessed whore, and I myself an arrant cuckold."

A "hobbadehoy" is a clumsy youth; the term was applied to Spadone, who was a young man chronologically, yet he was a boy due to being a eunuch.

A "dildo" is a foolish, inept boy; the term was applied to Nitido, the page.

Spadone said, "Truly, Secco, for the ancient good woman I dare swear point-blank; and the boy, surely, I always said, was to any man's thinking a very chrisome — innocent — in the thing you know. That's my opinion clearly."

Previously, he had done all he could to make Secco think that he was being cuckolded — while maintaining plausible deniability.

Clarella said to Secco, "What a wise goose-cap have thou showed thyself!"

Still convinced that he was a horned cuckold, Secco said to Morosa, "Here in my forehead it sticks, and stick it shall. Law I will have: I will never more tumble in sheets with thee, I will father no misbegotten child of thine; the court shall trounce thee, the city cashier thee, diseases devour thee, and the Spittle confound thee."

The Spittle is a hospital for the poor.

Secco exited.

"The man has dreamed himself into a lunacy," Castamela said.

"Alas, poor Nitido!" Silvia said.

"Truly, I am innocent," Nitido said.

"By the Virgin Mary, thou are; so thou are," Morosa said. "The world says how virtuously I have carried my good name in every part about me these threescore years and odd; and at last to slip with a child!

"There are men, men enough, tough and lusty, I hope, if one would give their mind to the iniquity of the flesh, but this is the life I have led with Secco for a while, since when he lies by me as cold as a dry stone."

Troylo-Savelli said, "This, ladies, is only a fit of novelty. All will be reconciled.

"I fear, Spadone, that your hand is in this here, however much you deny it."

Spadone said, "I deny it faithfully, in truth, indeed."

Troylo-Savelli said, "Well, well, enough.

"Morosa, be less troubled. This little disagreement is evidence of love, which will prove lasting. If Secco did not love you, he would not be so upset at thinking he has been cuckolded.

"Beauties, I attend you."

Everyone except Spadone and Nitido exited.

Spadone said, "Youngling, a word, youngling. Haven't you escaped the lash handsomely? Thank me for it."

Nitido said, "I fear thy roguery, and I shall find it."

"Is it possible?" Spadone said. "Give me thy little fist; we are friends. Have a care henceforth; remember this while you live."

He sang the words that Nitido had sang to him while teasing him about being a eunuch: "*And still the urchin would, but could not do.*"

He then said, "Pretty knave, and so forth; come, let's have a truce on all hands."

Nitido said, "Curse your fool's head; this was a jest in earnest."

— 4.2 —

No longer in disguise, Romanello stood alone in a room in his house.

He said to himself, "I will converse with beasts. There is in mankind no sound society. But in woman — bless me! — there is neither faith nor reason. I may justly wonder what trust was in my mother."

A servant entered the room and said, "A caroche, sir, stands at the gate."

A caroche is a luxurious coach.

Romanello said, "Let it stand still and freeze there! Make sure the locks —"

The servant said, "Too late; you have been forestalled."

Flavia, Romanello's sister, entered the room, followed by Camillo and Vespucci, who stood to the side.

Flavia said, "Brother, I have come —"

Romanello interrupted, "— unlooked for; I only sojourn myself."

He meant that he was staying there only temporarily.

He continued, "I keep neither house nor entertainments. French cooks' elaborate meals, Italian repasts, rich Persian feasts, with a train of servants performing services befitting exquisite ladies such as you are, do not perfume our low roofs."

His home did not smell of the odors of rich meals prepared for exquisite ladies; his was a temporary home, and he did not entertain in it.

Romanello continued, "The way for your exit lies open."

He pointed to the door and said, "That, there."

He then said, "Goodbye, great madam!"

"Why do you slight me?" Flavia, his sister, asked. "For what one act of mine, even from my childhood, which may deliver my deserts inferior either to our births or family, has natural affection become, in your contempt of me, a monster? What have I done for you to reject me like this?"

Vespucci whispered, "What is this, Camillo?"

Camillo whispered back, "It's not the usual style of conversation."

Romanello said, "I'm out of tune to chop discourse — to argue with you. You are, however, a woman."

Flavia said, "I am pensive and unfortunate, wanting and lacking a brother's bosom to disburden more griefs than female weakness can keep league with.

83

Let the worst malice, voiced in loud report, spit what it dares invent against my actions, and it shall never find a power to blemish my reputation other than beseems a patient, longsuffering person. I do not complain at lowness, and the fortunes that I attend on now are, as I value them, no new creation to a looser liberty."

She was saying that her morals had not changed.

She added, "Your strangeness may beget only a change in unreasonable opinion."

The very fact that he, her brother, was avoiding her was something that might cause an unfavorable opinion about her.

Camillo whispered, "Here's another tang — taste — of sense, Vespucci."

Vespucci whispered back, "Listen, and observe."

Romanello asked, "Aren't you, I ask you — nay, we'll be contented, in the presence of your ushers, once to prattle for some idle minutes — aren't you enthroned the lady-regent by whose special influence Julio, the Count of Camerine, is ordered?"

Flavia said, "It is known I am his wife, and in that title I am obedient to a service; else, the quiet of my wish was never ambitious of greatness."

She would have preferred staying married to her first husband.

"He loves you?" Romanello asked about Julio.

"As worthily as dearly," Flavia answered.

Romanello said, "And it is believed how practice quickly fashioned a port of humorous grotesqueness in carriage, discourse, demeanor, gestures."

He was saying that she was behaving grotesquely as the wife of Julio.

Camillo whispered, "That was put home roundly."

Vespucci whispered back, "What can be a ward for that blow?"

Flavia said, "Regard for the safety of my honor instructed me to practice such deceit."

Romanello asked, "The safety of your honor?"

Flavia pointed to Camillo and Vespucci and said, "Witness this brace — pair — of sprightly gallants, whose confederacy presumed to plot a siege."

She knew that they had plotted to seduce and share her.

Camillo and Vespucci said, "We, madam!"

Romanello said to his sister, "Go on. Go on. Some leisure serves us now."

Flavia said, "Always as Lord Julio pursued his contract with the man — oh, pardon me, if I forget to name him! — by whose poverty I was renounced of honest truth in marriage, these two, entrusted for a secret courtship, by tokens, letters, message, in their turns, offered their own devotions, as they termed them, almost to an impudence, regardless of him on whose support they relied."

As Julio was making arrangements with Flavia's husband to sell her to him, Julio had entrusted Camillo and Vespucci to secretly court Flavia for him. But both Camillo and Vespucci had courted her for themselves.

Romanello said to Camillo and Vespucci, "Don't dare for both your lives to interrupt her."

Flavia said, "Tormented thus to vexation, I assumed a dullness of simplicity; until afterwards, lost to my city-freedom, and now entered into this present state of my condition — marriage to Julio — concluding henceforth absolute security from their lascivious villainies, I continued my former custom of ridiculous lightness, as they continued their pursuit of me.

"To tell my lord about their actions would have ruined their best certainty of making a living. But that might yield suspicion in my nature. Women may be virtuous without mischief to such as tempt them."

She could have told Julio about the attempted seduction of her by both Camillo and Vespucci, but that would have lost them their jobs and might also have made Julio suspicious of her and made him wonder whether she was chaste.

By not telling Julio about Camillo and Vespucci, she had done them a kindness without being unvirtuous.

Romanello said to Camillo and Vespucci, "You are much to blame, sirs, should all that is truth be uttered."

Flavia said, "For that justice I did command them hither; for a privacy in conversation between Flavia and her brother needed no secretaries such as these are.

"Now, Romanello, thou are every refuge I fly for justice to; if I am thy sister, and not a bastard, answer their confession, or threaten vengeance, with perpetual silence."

In other words: Punish them if and as you wish, but don't talk about it later.

Camillo said, "My follies are acknowledged; you're a lady who has outdone the model of chastity. When I trespass in anything except duty and respects of service, may hopes of joys forsake me!"

Vespucci said, "To like penance I join a constant votary."

Both men were vowing to reform.

A votary is bound by a vow to live a religious life.

Romanello said, "Peace, then, is ratified."

He accepted their vows to reform, and so he would not mete out punishment to them.

He continued, "My sister, thou have wakened entranced affection from its sleep to knowledge of once more who thou are. No jealous frenzy shall hazard a distrust: Reign in thy sweetness, thou only-worthy woman. These two converts record our hearty union. I have shaken off my thralldom, lady, and I have made discoveries of famous innovations and novelties, but of those I will speak later. Thus we seal love: you shall know all, and wonder."

Romanello and Flavia were now reconciled as brother and sister.

Livio entered the room and said, "Health and his heart's desire to Romanello! I bring my welcome with me."

He was bringing what he considered good news: That was his welcome.

Livio then said to Flavia, "Noblest lady, excuse an ignorance of your fair presence; this may be held to be an intrusion."

"Not by me, sir," Flavia said.

Romanello said, "You are not frequently a guest here, as I remember. But since you bring your welcome with you, Livio, be bold to use it: Get to the point."

Livio said, "This lady, with both these gentlemen, in happy hour may be partakers of the long-lived amity our souls must link in."

Romanello said, "So; it is likely that the Marquis Octavio stores some new grace, some special secret employment, for whom your kind commendations, by deputation, it pleases you to think to oblige; and Livio's charity descends on Romanello liberally, above my means to thank!"

Livio said, "Octavio, the Marquis of Siena, at some past time has been informed how gladly there did pass a treaty of chaste loves with Castamela."

He meant a chaste love between Romanello and Castamela.

Livio continued, "From this good heart, I say that it was in me an error, willful and without cause, it is confessed, that hindered such honorable prosecution, even and equal: Better thoughts consider how much I wronged the gentle course that led you to vows of true affection, as of friendship."

In a way, Livio had prevented Castamela from agreeing to marry Romanello. Livio had brought her to Octavio's palace. He had worried about finances and had communicated that worry to her.

Romanello thought, *Sits the wind there, boy!*

He was scenting a trick.

Romanello said, "Setting formal circumstances aside, proceed; you dally yet."

In other words: Get to the point.

Livio said, "Then, without plea, for countenancing what has been injurious on my part, I have come to really tender my sister as a loved wife to you; freely take her, you very honest man; and as you live together, may your increase of years prove just one spring — one lasting flourishing youth! She is your own. My hands shall accomplish what's required for the ceremony."

Couples could join hands and vow to marry each other. This was a binding agreement.

Livio may have meant that he would take their hands and join them together, or he may meant that he would pay for the wedding and the wedding feast.

"Brother, this day was meant to be a holiday for feasting on every side," Flavia said.

Romanello said, "The newly become courtier offers most frankly, but indeed he leaves out a due consideration of the narrowness our short estate is bounded in: My wealth is meager.

"Some politicians, as they rise up, like Livio, to perfection, in their own sufficiency for living well, gather also a grave supplement of foresight and wisdom, yet Livio falls short in his.

"You triumph and exult in your advantages; it smells of politics.

"We know you are no fool."

Flavia said, "Indeed, I believe him."

Camillo said, "Else it would be willful deception — willful fraud."

Vespucci said, "It would be rank and senseless folly."

Livio said, "Ask me to swear an oath at large. I will swear it."

Romanello said, "Since you are in earnest, receive this in satisfaction: I'm resolved to live a single life. There was a time, Livio, when indiscretion blinded foresight in me, but recollection of my lack of wealth, and your rules of thriftiness, prevailed against all passion."

Livio said, "You'd be courted. Courtship's the child of coyness, Romanello, and as for the rules, it is possible to name them."

By "name them," he may have meant that it was possible to create and name new rules.

Romanello quoted some words that Livio had said earlier when Romanello wanted to marry Castamela: "A single life's no burden; but to draw in yokes is chargeable, and will require a double maintenance."

He then said, "Those are Livio's exact words. And he said this: 'Why, I can live without a wife and purchase.'"

"Purchase" is annual income from property. Such property may make up a wife's dowry.

Or maybe Romanello quoted Livio as saying, "Why, I can live without a wife, and purchase."

If that is what he said, then he meant that he could live without a wife and could purchase an estate.

Romanello continued, "By our lady the Virgin Mary, so you do, sir; may God send you joy for it! These rules, you see, are possible, and answered."

He meant that Livio had made some rules — the ones that Romanello had just quoted — that were feasible and that Romanello was returning in answer to him.

Livio said, "A full answer was recently made to this already: My sister's only thine."

Why would Livio be so anxious to have Romanello marry his sister? Romanello was still as lacking in wealth as he had been before when Livio was opposed to the marriage.

One answer could be that Castamela had become unchaste and needed to be married to save her reputation. Livio may believe that. So could Romanello.

Romanello replied, "Where lives the creature — Castamela — your pity stoops to pin upon your servant — me?

"Not in a nunnery for a year's probation. No such coldness for her!

"There are Bowers of Fancies ravished from troops of fairy nymphs, and virgins culled from the downy breasts of queens their mothers, in the empire of the Titans, far from mortals.

"But these are tales: Truly, I have quite abandoned all loving humor."

"Here is scorn in riddles," Livio said.

Romanello said, "If there were another Marquis in Siena more powerful than the same who is vicegerent to the Great Duke of Florence, our grand master ...

"If the Great Duke himself were here, and would lift up my head to fellow-pomp among his nobles by falsehood to the honor of a sister, urging me to be an instrument in his seraglio ...

"I'd tear the wardrobe of an outside from him, rather than live as a pander to his bribery."

"Seraglio" is the name of the women's apartments in a palace of the Ottomans. Another name for the women's apartments is a harem.

Romanello was accusing Livio of selling his sister to Octavio.

Livio said, "So would the man you are talking to, Romanello, without making such a singular noise as you are now making."

Anticipating that Livio would now criticize his — Romanello's — sister, Romanello said, "Flavia is a countess, she is; but she has an Earl as her husband, though he is far from our procurement."

Romanello had not procured Julio to be his sister's husband; he had had nothing to do with the marriage.

A procurer is a pimp.

Livio asked, "Castamela is refused, then? You will not marry her?"

Romanello said, "She was never appointed as my choice."

He had previously wanted to marry her, but she had never been officially made his choice, as she would have been if she had agreed to marry him.

He continued, "You know, and I know, Livio — more, I tell thee, a noble honesty ought to make allowances when reason intercedes. By all that's manly, I say these words not in derision, but in compassion."

Livio said, "Intelligence flies swiftly."

The intelligence was gossip that Castamela had become a Fancy.

Romanello said, "Pretty swiftly. We have compared the copy with the original, and find no disagreement."

The original was Castamela then when Romanello wanted to marry her, and the copy was Castamela now when Romanello did not want to marry her. Back then Castamela had been concerned about wealth, and now Castamela was concerned about wealth. For all Romanello knew, she had become a Fancy out of concern about material prosperity.

Livio said, "So my sister can be no wife for Romanello?"

Romanello said, "No, no. One no, once more and forever.

"This courtesy of yours deceived me for a second.

"Sir, you brought a welcome. You must not depart without it. Scan with pity my plainness: I intend neither anger nor quarrel."

Livio replied, "Far be it from me to press a blame."

He then said to Flavia, "Great lady, I kiss your noble hands, and to these gentlemen" — he meant Camillo and Vespucci — "I present a civil parting."

He then said, 'Romanello, by the next foot-messenger thou will hear some news of alteration."

The alteration could be a change in his circumstances and in his relationships to others. For example, it could be an invitation to duel.

Livio added, "If I send for you, come to me."

Romanello said, "Without question, I will."

Livio said, "My thanks may requite the favor."

He exited.

Flavia said, "Brother, his exchange of conversation appears at once perplexed, but yet sensible."

Romanello said, "These doubts are easily resolved.

"Upon your virtues the whole foundation of my peace is grounded. I'll escort you to your home. Lost in one comfort, here I have found another."

He had lost a possible marriage to Castamela, but he had been reconciled with his sister.

Flavia said, "May Goodness prosper it!"

CHAPTER 5

— 5.1 —

Octavio, Troylo-Savelli, Secco, and Nitido met in an apartment in the palace.

Octavio said, "No more of these complaints and clamors! Have we neither enemies abroad nor waking sycophants, who, peering through our actions, await an opportunity for which they watch to lay an opportunity open to vulgar talk, but among ourselves, some whom we call our own must practice scandal out of a liberty of ease and fullness against our honor? We shall quickly order an extreme re-establishment of peace, sirs, and you will find it."

He wanted peace in the palace. There were enemies and sycophants waiting for an opportunity to strike, and lack of peace in the palace might give them that opportunity. To anyone not keeping the peace, he would give an extreme punishment.

Troylo-Savelli said, "When servants' servants, aka slaves, once relish license of good opinion from a noble nature — that is, being in the good graces of their master — they take upon themselves the boldness to abuse such interest, and lord it over their fellows, as if they were exempt from that condition of servitude."

Octavio replied, "He who doesn't know how to rule at home his household is unfit to manage public matters."

He then said to Secco, "You must be jealous, you puppy! And of a boy, too!"

A puppy is a foolish young boy or man. The boy was Nitido.

Octavio continued:

"You raise uproars and bandy noise among young maidens.

"You keep revels in your madness.

"You use the authority of giving punishment.

"A fool must fool you.

"And this is all only a pastime to you — so you think!"

Nitido said, "With your good lordship's favor, since then, Spadone has confessed that it was a trick put on Secco to get some revenge meant for me."

Troylo-Savelli said, "He vowed it to be the truth before the ladies, in my hearing."

Octavio replied, "Sirrah, I'll turn you again to your shop and trinkets, your suds and pan of charcoal. Take your damsel, the grand old rag of beauty, your death's-head, and try then what business reverence can trade in. Fiddle, and play your pranks among your neighbors, so that you may roar throughout all the town. Now you simper and look like a shaved skull."

Nitido said, "This is what comes from prating — from talking idly."

Secco said, "I am, my lord, a worm. Please, my lord, tread on me. I will not turn again. Alas, I shall never venture to hang my barber pole out, on my knees I beg it, on my bare knees. I will go down before my wife, and do what she will have me do, all I can do. Nay, more, if she will have it, I will ask for her forgiveness, be an obedient husband, and never cross her, unless sometimes in kindness.

"Seignior Troylo, speak one sweet word for me. I'll swear it was in my madness. I said I knew not what, and I'll swear that you brought no creature among the ladies.

"Nitido, I'll forswear thee, too."

He had previously sworn that Troylo-Savelli and Nitido had brought Prugnuolo (the disguised Romanello) among the ladies. Now he was prepared to swear that they had not done that.

Octavio said, "Wait awhile our pleasure. You shall know more soon."

Secco replied, "Remember me now."

Secco and Nitido exited.

Octavio said, "Troylo, thou are my brother's son, and you are nearest in blood to me; thou have been next in counsels. Those ties of nature (if thou can consider how much they do engage) work by instinct in every worthy or ignoble comment that can concern me."

Because Troylo-Savelli was a close relative who advised him, he shared whatever reputation — good or bad — that Octavio acquired.

Troylo-Savelli said, "Sir, those ties of nature have done that, and they shall, as long as I bear life."

Octavio said, "From henceforth the stewardship that my carefulness for the honor of our family has undertaken must yield the world account and make clear reckonings; but now we stand suspected of having done evil in our just and even courses of action."

Using the majestic plural, he was saying that he had been acting ethically, but he had learned — from Castamela — that she, and no doubt others, suspected him of having behaved unethically concerning his stewardship of the three Fancies.

Because Troylo-Savelli was so close to him, he was also implicated in the imputation of bad conduct.

Troylo-Savelli said, "But when time shall wonder at how much it was mistaken in the issue of honorable and secure arrangements for the three Fancies, your wisdom, crowned with laurels of a justice deserving approbation, will quite foil the ignorance of popular opinion."

Octavio said, "Gossip is merry with my feats; my dotage, undoubtedly, the vulgar voices sing it like a carol."

Troylo-Savelli said, "True, sir; but Romanello's late admission while in disguise to the Fancies warrants that giddy confidence of gossip without all contradiction.

"Now Romanello is regarded as true as an oracle, and he is so received by all: I am confirmed that the lady Castamela by this time has proven to be Romanello's scorn as well as a cause of his laughter."

Octavio said, "And we along with her are the topics of his table-talk. Does she stand in any firm affection to him?"

Troylo-Savelli said, "None, sir, no more than her usual nobleness afforded out of a civil custom."

He meant that Castamela had good manners and was polite to Romanello, but she had no special liking for him.

Octavio said, "We are resolute in our determination, and we intend quickly to cause these clouds of approbation to fly off; the arranging of it, nephew, is thine."

Troylo-Savelli said, "Your care and love command me."

Livio entered the room and said, "I come to you, my lord, as a petitioner."

Octavio said, "Honest Livio, you are perfectly honest, really; no fallacies and no flaws are in thy truth. I shall promote thee to a more eminent position."

Troylo-Savelli said, "Livio deserves it."

Octavio said, "What is thy petition to me? Speak boldly."

Livio said, "Please, discharge me from my position as master of your horse. It would be better to live as a yeoman, and live with men, than oversee your horses, while I myself am ridden like a jade."

A jade is a bad horse.

A yeoman has a small estate.

If Livio were to cease being master of the horse and become a yeoman, his social status would be much lower. But according to him, he would be treated much more respectfully.

Livio's words were insulting to Octavio.

Octavio said, "Such words sound like only ill manners. Know, young man, old as we are, our soul retains a fire that is active and quick in motion, which shall equal the most daring boy's ambition of true manhood who wears a pride to defy us."

Troylo-Savelli said to Octavio about Livio, "He's my friend, sir."

He did not want them to fight a duel.

"You're weary of our service, and may leave it," Octavio said to Livio. "We can court no man's duty."

Livio said, "Without passion, my lord, do you think that your nephew here, your Troylo, partakes in your spirit as freely as he partakes in your blood?"

Octavio had spirit: courage. Livio was asking if Troylo-Savelli had courage. Apparently, he was seeking to challenge Troylo-Savelli to fight.

Livio added, "It is not a rude question."

He meant that he had grounds for asking that.

Thinking that Livio was implying that Troylo-Savelli was illegitimate, Octavio replied, "If you had known his mother, you might have sworn that she is honest. Let him prove that he is not base-born. For thy sister's sake, I do conceive the like of thee; be wiser, but prate to me no more like this."

Octavio was OK with Troylo-Savelli and Livio fighting a duel.

He then said to Troylo-Savelli, "If this gallant is resolved on my attendance, before he leaves me, acquaint him with the present service, nephew, I meant to employ him in."

He exited.

Troylo-Savelli said, "Bah, Livio, why have you turned wild suddenly?"

Livio said, "Pretty gentleman, how modestly you plead your fears! How tamely!

"Ask Romanello; he has, without permission, surveyed your Bowers of Fancies, and he has discovered the mystery of those pure nuns, those chaste ones — untouched, indeed! The holy academy!

"He has found a mother's daughter there of mine, too, and one who called my father 'father'; he talks about it, ruffles in mirth about it; he disgraced to my face the glory of her greatness by it."

Troylo-Savelli asked, "Truly?"

Livio said, "Death to my sufferance, can thou hear this misery, and answer it with a 'truly'? It was thy wickedness, as false as thine own heart, which tempted my credulity and brought her to ruin.

"She was once an innocent, as free from sin as the blue face of Heaven without a cloud in it; she is now as sullied as is that canopy when mists and vapors separate it from our sight and threaten pestilence."

This society believed that breathing in mists and vapors was unhealthy and caused disease.

Troylo-Savelli asked, "Does Romanello say so, Livio?"

Livio answered, "Yes, if your nobleness likes it, he truly does say so.

"Your breach of friendship with me must borrow courage from your uncle, while your sword talks an answer. There's no remedy: I will have satisfaction, although thy life becomes short because of such a demand."

He was challenging Troylo-Savelli to a duel.

Troylo-Savelli replied, "Then satisfaction, much worthier than your sword can force, you shall have, yet my sword shall keep the peace and remain undrawn. I can be angry, and speak boasts aloud in my reply; but honor schools me to fitter grounds. This, as a gentleman, I promise, before the minutes of the night warn us to rest, you will hear such satisfaction from me, and credit it as such you cannot wish better than. The satisfaction shall be so good that you cannot think of any better satisfaction."

Livio said, "Cannot? The time is short. Before our sleeping hour, you vow?"

Troylo-Savelli replied, "I do. Before we ought to sleep."

Livio said, "So I understand you to mean.

"Having confidence in what you say, I ask what the Marquis wanted me to do? I'll do it."

Troylo-Savelli said, "Invite Count Julio, his lady, and her brother, with their company, to my lord's court at supper."

Julio's lady was his wife: Flavia. Her brother, of course, was Romanello.

Livio said, "That's an easy business. And then —"

Troylo-Savelli interrupted, "And then, soon after, the performance of my just-now-made vow to you will occur, but be certain that you bring these guests with you."

Livio said, "I am still your servant."

Troylo-Savelli said, "You are more than that — you are my friend. You'll find that you are no less to me."

Livio said, "This is strange. Is it possible?"

Castamela and the three Fancies — Clarella, Floria, and Silvia — spoke together in another room in the palace.

Castamela said, "You have discoursed to me a lovely story. My heart dances to the music; it would be a sin if I would in any tittle stand distrustful, where such a people, such as you are, innocent even by the authority of your years and language, inform a truth.

"Oh, say it over again!

"You are, you say, three daughters of one mother. That mother was the only sister to the Marquis Octavio, whose responsibility has, since her death, being left a 'widow,' here in this place provided your education."

In this society, the word "widow" could mean "widower." Octavio was figuratively a widower since he had assumed responsibility for these children whose mother — his sister — had died; that is, he resembled a widow or widower. Therefore, he had raised and educated his nieces.

Castamela asked, "Is that so?"

Clarella said, "It is even so; and howsoever gossip may wander loosely in some scandal against our privacies, yet we have lacked no graceful means fit for our births and qualities, to educate us up into a virtuous knowledge of what and who we ought to be."

Floria said, "Our uncle has often told us how it more concerned him, before he showed us to the world, to render our youths and our demeanors in each action tested and approved by his experience, than allow us to too early adventure on the follies of the age, which because of easy temptations is deadly."

Silvia said, "In good deed, we mean no harm."

Castamela said, "Deceit must lack a shelter under a roof that's covering to souls so white as breathe beneath it, such as these souls of yours are. My happiness shares largely in this blessing, and I must thank the direction of the providence that led me hither."

Clarella said, "Aptly have you named its providence; for always in chaste loves such majesty has power. Our kinsman Troylo-Savelli was herein his own agent; he will prove — believe him, lady — in every way as constant and loyal as he is noble. We can bail him from the cruelty of misunderstanding."

Floria said, "You will find his tongue only a just secretary to his heart."

Castamela said, "Dear creatures, the female guardian, Morosa, now and then, it seems, makes bold to talk."

Clarella said, "She has waited on us from all our cradles, and she will prate sometimes oddly; however, she means only entertainment. I am unwilling that our household should break up, but I must obey his wisdom under whose command we live. Sever our companies I'm sure we shall not. This is still a pretty and quiet life."

Morosa and Secco entered the room. Secco was wearing his barber's apron and carried his barber's equipment: a basin of water, scissors, comb, towels, razor, etc.

Secco said to Morosa, his wife, "Chuck, duckling, honey, mouse, monkey, all and everything, I am thine forever and only. I will never offend again, as I hope to shave cleanly, and get honor by it. Heartily I ask for thy forgiveness; be gracious to thine own flesh and blood, and kiss me home."

Morosa said, "Look that you provoke us no more, for this time you shall find mercy. Was it that hedgehog that set thy brains a-crowing? Be quits with him, but do not hurt the great male-baby."

The hedgehog was Spadone; the great male-baby was Nitido.

Secco replied, "Enough. I am wise, and I will be merry."

He then said to Castamela and the three Fancies, "Make haste, beauties; the caroches will quickly receive you. A night of pleasure is at hand; pray for good husbands for each of you, so that they may trim you skillfully, dainty ones, and let me alone to trim them."

Two meanings of "trim you" are "make you pregnant" and "have sex with you." Another meaning is relevant to barbers.

Morosa said, "Loving hearts, be quick as soon as you can; time runs apace."

Some of her words had a bawdy meaning. "Be quick as soon as you can" can mean "Be pregnant as soon as you can." She seemed to be advocating *carpe diem*.

She continued, "What you must do, do nimbly, and give your minds to it. Young bloods stand fumbling!"

Again, she seemed to be advocating that the young ladies have sex. Young men stand — have an erection — and masturbate.

She continued, "Bah, go! Be ready, for shame, beforehand.

"Husband, stand to thy equipment, husband, like a man of mettle."

A husband can stand — have an erection — like a man of metal.

Morosa said, "Go, go, go!"

She exited with Castamela and the three Fancies.

Secco said aloud, "Will you come away, loiterers? Shall I wait all day? Am I your servant, do you think?"

Spadone and Nitido entered the room. Spadone was ready to get a haircut and a shave.

Spadone said, "Here I am, and I am ready. What a loud mouthing thou make! I have just scoured my hands and curried my head to save time. Honest Secco! Neat Secco! Precious barbarian! Now thou look like a worshipful, honorable puller of teeth."

This was another duty of barbers in society.

He added, "I wish that I might see thee on horseback in the pomp once!"

As a barber, Secco might ride in a procession of the city companies of trades and callings.

Secco said, "A chair! A chair! Quick! Quick!"

Nitido said, "Here's a chair, a chair-politic — an ingenious chair — my fine boy. Sit thee down in triumph, and rise as one of the Nine Worthies."

The Nine Worthies were nine great men: three from the Bible, three from classical times, and three from romances. The three from the Bible were Joshua, King David, and Judas Maccabaeus. The three from classical times were Hector of Troy, Alexander the Great, and Julius Caesar. The three from romances were King Arthur, Holy Roman Emperor Charlemagne, and Godfrey of Bouillon.

Nitido continued, "Thou shall be a sweet youth soon, sirrah."

Spadone sat down in the chair and said, "So go to work with a grace now. I cannot but highly be in love with the fashion of gentry, which is never complete until the snip-snap of dexterity has mowed-off the excrements of slovenry."

In this society, hairs were called "excrements."

As he massaged Spadone's scalp, Secco said about Spadone's use of words, "Very commodiously delivered, I say."

Nitido said to Secco, "Nay, the thing under your fingers is a whelp of the wits, I can assure you."

A whelp is a puppy. Used to refer to an adult man, the term is contemptuous.

Spadone objected, "I a whelp of the wits! No, no, I cannot bark impudently and ignorantly enough. Oh, if a man of this barber's art had now and then sovereignty over fair ladies, you would tickle their upper and their lower lips, you'd so smouch and belaver their chops!"

To "smouch" means to "kiss loudly." To "lave" means to "wash." A person's chops are that person's mouth.

Secco said, "We light on some offices for ladies, too, as opportunity serves."

Nitido said, "Yes; frizzle or powder their hair, pluck their eyebrows, set a layer of powder on their cheeks, keep secrets, and tell gossip; that's all."

Secco told Spadone, "Shut quickly both your eyes. The ingredients to the composition of this ball are most odorous camphor, pure soap of Venice, oil of sweet-almonds, with the spirit of alum. They will search and smart shrewdly, if you don't keep the shop-windows of your head closed."

Spadone shut his eyes while Secco smeared his whole face.

Spadone said, "Gossip! That's well remembered: That's part of your trade, too — please do not rub so roughly — and how goes the tattle of the town? What novelties are stirring, ha?"

Secco said, "They are strange, and scarcely to be believed. A gelding was lately seen to leap on an old mare in the equine sexual position; and an old man of one hundred and twelve stood in a white sheet for getting a wench of fifteen pregnant here hard by — that is, nearby. Most admirable and portentous!"

Spadone said, "I'll never believe it; it is impossible."

"It is most certain," Nitido said. "Some doctor-farriers are of opinion that the mare may cast a foal that the master of their hall concludes, in spite of all jockeys and their familiar friends, will carry every race before him without spur or switch."

Farriers trim and shoe the hooves of horses.

Spadone said, "Oh, splendid! A man might venture — gamble — ten or twenty to one safely then, and never be in danger of the cheat."

He then said, "This water, I think, is none of the sweetest; it's camphor and soap of Venice, did you say?"

"With a little Grecum album for mundification," Secco replied.

"Mundification" is "the act of cleaning a wound."

Nitido said, "Grecum album is a kind of white perfumed powder, which plain country-people, I believe, call dog-musk."

Musk need not smell particularly pleasant.

"Dog-musk!" Spadone said. "A pox on the dog-musk! What! Do thou mean to bleach my nose, thou who give such twitches to it? Set me at liberty as soon as thou can, gentle Secco."

The audience may wonder whether Spadone's arms are restrained in the ingenious chair.

Secco said, "I need only pare off a little superfluous down from your chin, and all's done."

Spadone said, "Pish, there's no need for that; finish, I entreat thee."

"Have patience, man," Nitido said. "It is for Secco's credit to be neat."

Spadone said, "What is that thing that is so cold at my throat and scrubs so hard?"

Secco said, "A kind of steel instrument called a razor, a sharp and keen tool. It has a certain virtue of cutting a throat, if a man should please to give his mind to it.

"Hold up your muzzle, Seignior."

Secco and Nitido were and had been using canine terminology to refer to Spadone.

Secco continued, "When did you last talk bawdily to my wife? Tell me, for your own good, Seignior, I advise you."

Spadone said, "I talk bawdily to thy wife! Hang bawdry!"

"Good man, now, mind thy business and be careful, lest thy hand slip."

Nitido said, "Give him kind words, you were best, on account of a trifle that I know."

Secco said, "Confess, or I shall mar your grace in whiffing tobacco, or the squirting of sweet wines down your gullet."

He was ready and willing to cut Spadone's throat and make it difficult for Spadone to smoke tobacco or to drink wine. That was the trifle that Nitido knew.

Secco added, "You have been offering to play the gelding we told you of, I suppose."

He was referring to the gelding horse that had leaped on an old mare.

"Speak the truth; move the semicircle of your countenance to my left-hand side."

The semicircles of a face are the eyebrows.

Secco had either shaved one of Spadone's eyebrows off or had covered it with "soap."

Secco continued, "Out with the truth: Would you have had a sexual leap on my wife?"

Nitido said, "Spadone, thou are in a lamentable pickle. Have a good heart, and pray if thou can. I pity thee."

Spadone said, "I profess and vow, friend Secco, that I know no leaps, I."

"Lecherously goatish, and a eunuch!" Secco said. "This cut, and then —"

One meaning of "cut" is "vulva."

Spadone said, "Confound thee, thy leaps and thy cuts! I am no eunuch, you finical — affected — ass. I am no eunuch, but at all points I am as well provided as any man in Italy, and thy wife could have told thee that. This is your conspiracy! To thrust my head into a brazen tub of kitchen-lye, hoodwink — blind — my eyes in mud-soap, and then attempt to cut my throat in the dark, like a coward! I may live to be revenged on both of you."

Nitido said, "Oh, scurvy! Thou are angry. Feel, man, whether thy weason — windpipe — is not cracked first."

Secco said, "You must fiddle my brains into a jealousy, rub my temples with saffron, and burnish — polish — my forehead with the juice of yellows!"

In this society, yellow is the color of jealousy.

He then asked, "Have I fitted you now, sir? Have I given you a fit?"

Morosa entered the room.

Spadone said, "All's whole yet, I hope."

He meant that he hoped his throat had not been cut, and perhaps that his sexual equipment was still whole.

Morosa said, "Yes, sirrah, all is whole yet; but if thou ever speak treason against my sweeting and me once more, thou shall find a rogue-y, vile bargain of it."

She then said to her husband, "Dear, this was handled like one of spirit and discretion."

She added, "Nitido has paged it trimly, too.

"No wording and talking, but get ready and attend at court."

Secco said to Spadone, "Now that we know thou are a man, we forget what has passed, and we are fellows and friends again."

Nitido said, "Wipe your face clean, and take heed of — beware of — a razor."

Morosa, Secco, and Nitido exited.

Spadone said, "My fear put me into a sweat; I cannot help it. I am glad I still have my throat for my own, and I must either laugh to be sociable or be laughed at."

Livio and Troylo-Savelli spoke together in a stateroom in the palace.

Livio said, "You see, sir, that I have proven to be a ready servant, and I have brought the expected guests amid these feastings, these costly entertainments. You must pardon my incivility that here sequesters your ears from your choice of music or discourse to a less pleasant parley. Night draws on, and quickly will grow old. It would be unmanly for any gentleman who loves his honor to put it on the rack and stretch out the time before redeeming it.

"Here so far is small comfort of such a satisfaction as was promised to me by you, although certainly it must be had.

"Please tell me, what can appear about me to make me be treated like this? My soul is free from injuries."

Troylo-Savelli said, "My tongue is free from serious untruths; I never wronged you, I love and respect you too well to mean to wrong you now."

Livio said, "You have not wronged me? Blessed Heaven! This is abuse of a patience beyond all endurance."

Troylo-Savelli said, "If your own acknowledgment won't acquit me fairly, then before the hours of rest shall shut our eyes up for sleep, say I made a forfeit of what no length of years can once redeem."

Livio said, "These are fine whirls in tame imagination! Go on, sir! It is scarcely mannerly at such a season, such a ceremony, the place and presence considered, to mix combustions with delights."

Troylo-Savelli said, "Prepare for free and honorable contentments, and give them welcome."

Trumpets sounded the arrival of an important person, and Octavio entered the showroom, accompanied by Julio, Flavia, Romanello, and Julio's attendants Camillo and Vespucci.

Octavio said to Julio, "I dare not study words, or observe formal courtesies, for this particular, this special favor."

He was thanking Julio for being his guest, and he was saying that neither words nor formal courtesies were enough to thank him properly.

Julio said, "Your bounty and your love, my lord, must justly engage our thankfulness."

Flavia said, "Indeed, the varieties of entertainment here have so exceeded all account of plenty, that you have left, great sir, no splendors except an equal welcome, which may purchase the reputation of a similar hospitality."

She was saying that Julio and she needed to give Octavio the same welcome and hospitality that he had given to them.

Octavio said, "But for this grace, madam, I will lay open before your judgment, which I know can rate and value them, a cabinet of rich and lively jewels — the world can show none better — that I prize as dearly as I prize my life."

He then called, "Nephew!"

Already knowing what he was to do, Troylo-Savelli said, "Sir, I obey you."

He exited.

Flavia asked, "Jewels, my lord?"

Octavio replied, "No stranger's eye has ever viewed them, unless your brother Romanello by chance was wooed to a sight for his approval — no more."

Romanello said, "Not I, I do protest. I hope, sir, you cannot think I am a lapidary. I have skill in jewels!"

A lapidary is a jeweler, and/or a person who cuts and polishes gemstones, and/or a person who is a connoisseur of jewelry.

Octavio said, "It is a proper quality for any gentleman."

Referring to Julio's attendants Camillo and Vespucci, he added, "Your other friends, maybe, are not so coy and shy."

"Who, they?" Julio said. "They can't tell a topaz from an opal."

Camillo admitted, "We are ignorant in gems that are not common."

Vespucci added, "But his lordship is pleased, it seems, to test our ignorance to pass the time until the jewels are brought here.

"Please, look upon a letter recently sent to me.

"Lord Julio, madam, Romanello, read a novelty. It is written from Bologna.

"Fabricio, once a merchant in this city, has entered into religious orders, and has been received among the Capuchins as a fellow; this is news that ought not in any way to be unpleasant.

"This news is certainly true, I can assure you."

Fabricio had reformed, as he had promised, and he had become a Capuchin monk. He had gone from being a spendthrift to taking a vow of voluntary poverty.

Julio said, "He at last has bestowed himself upon a glorious service."

"Most happy man!" Romanello said.

He said to his sister, who had been married to Fabricio, "I now forgive him for the injuries thy former life exposed thee to."

Livio, who was unhappy with his life, thought, *Turn Capuchin! He! While I stand a cipher — a zero! — and fill up only an useless sum to be paid out in an unthrifty lewdness, that must buy both name and riot — both reputation and debauchery! Oh, my fickle destiny!*

Using the metaphor of tasting food, Romanello said, "Sister, you cannot taste this course but excellently, and thankfully."

Literally, the course was a course of action.

Flavia said, "He's now dead to the world, and he now lives to Heaven; may a saint's reward reward him!"

She thought, *My only loved lord, all your fears are henceforth confined to a sweet and happy penance.*

Troylo-Savelli returned, leading the "jewels," who were Castamela and the three Fancies: Clarella, Floria, and Silvia. Morosa, their female guardian, accompanied them.

Octavio said, "Behold, I keep my word; these are the jewels that deserve a treasury. I can be prodigal among my friends. Examine well their luster. Doesn't it sparkle? Why does your silence dwell in such amazement?"

Livio thought, *Patience, keep within me. Don't rudely leap yet into the scorn of anger.*

Flavia said, "They are incomparable beauties!"

Octavio said, "Romanello, I have been only the steward of your pleasures. You loved this lady once; what do you say to her now?"

Castamela said to Romanello, "I must not court you, sir."

Romanello replied, "By no means, fair one. Enjoy your life of greatness. Surely, the spring is past, the Bower of Fancies is quite withered, and it is offered like a lottery to be drawn. I dare not venture for a lottery ticket. Excuse me."

He said sarcastically, "Exquisite jewels!"

Both Livio and Romanello believed that Castamela and the three Fancies were unchaste.

"Listen, Troylo," Livio said.

"Spare me," Troylo-Savelli replied.

Octavio said, "You, then, renounce all right in Castamela? Say the truth, Romanello."

"Gladly," Romanello replied.

"Then I must not," Troylo-Savelli said.

He hugged Castamela and said, "Thus I embrace my own, my wife."

He said to her, "Confirm it thus. When I fail, my dearest, to deserve thee, may comforts and life fail me!"

He wanted to marry her. By "When I fail …," he meant, "If I should ever fail …."

Castamela said, "I make the same vow, I do, for my part."

Troylo-Savelli said, "To Livio, who is now my brother-in-law, I have justly given satisfaction."

Castamela said to her brother, "Oh, excuse our secrecy; I have been —"

Livio finished the sentence for her: "— much more worthy of a better brother, and he — Troylo-Savelli — is a better friend than my dull brains could fashion."

Romanello asked, "Have I been deceived?"

Octavio answered, "You have not, Romanello. We examined on what conditions your affections fixed, and found them merely courtship, but my nephew loved with a resolved faith, and used his prudent policy to draw the lady into this society, more freely to reveal his sincerity, even without Livio's knowledge. And thus my nephew succeeded and prospered: he's my heir, and she deserved him."

Julio said to Romanello, "Don't storm at what is past."

Flavia said, "A fate as happy may crown you with a full measure of content."

Octavio said, "Despite whatever gossip has stated abroad about me and these Fancies, know they are all my nieces. They are the daughters to my dead sole sister; this woman, Morosa, has been their female guardian since they first saw the world. Indeed, my mistresses they are, I have none other; how they have been brought up, their qualities may speak."

In this society, a mistress could be a woman who is loved with no sexual desire.

Octavio continued, "Now, Romanello and gentlemen, for such I know you all, portions — dowries — both fit and worthy they shall not lack nor will I look on fortune."

He meant that in their choice of husbands he would not consider their suitors' wealth or lack of it.

He continued, "If you like, court them and win them; here is free access in my own court henceforth. Only for thee, Livio, I wish my niece Clarella were allotted to be thy wife."

"Most noble lord, I am struck silent," Livio said.

Flavia said, "Brother, here's a noble choice of potential wives."

Romanello said, "Frenzy, how did thou seize me!"

The ancient Romans sometimes blamed Furor, goddess of frenzy, when they committed something ill advised and rash.

Clarella said to him, "We knew who you were, sir, when you were disguised as Prugnuolo."

"We were merry at the sight," Floria said.

"And we gave you welcome," Silvia said.

"Indeed, truly, and so we did, if you like," Morosa said.

"Enough, enough," Octavio said. "Now, to end the night, some domestic servants of my own are ready to present a merriment; they intend, according to the occasion of the meeting, in several types of characters, to show how love over-sways all men of several conditions: soldier, member of the gentry, fool, scholar, merchantman, and countryman. This is a harmless recreation.

"Take your places."

Music sounded.

Spadone, Secco, Nitido, and three other dancers wearing masks, dressed respectively as a soldier, a member of the gentry, a fool, a scholar, a merchant, and a countryman, entered and danced.

After the dance was over, Octavio said to the maskers, "Your duties have been performed.

"Henceforth, Spadone, cast aside thy borrowed title of eunuch. The mother of my nephew Troylo breastfed thee: Esteem him honestly.

"Lights for the lodgings!"

He was calling for servants to escort them to their rooms with candles. Octavio then said:

"It is high time for rest.

"Great men may be misunderstood when they mean best."

EPILOGUE

Morosa said:

"Awhile suspected, gentlemen, I look

"For no new law, being quitted [acquitted] by the book [the play]."

Clarella said:

"Our harmless pleasures free in every sort

"Actions of scandal; may they free report!

[May they absolve the dishonorable reports of our actions!]"

Castamela said:

"Distrust is base, presumption urges wrongs;

"But noble thoughts must prompt as noble tongues."

Flavia said:

"Fancy and judgment are a play's full matter:

"If we have erred in one, right you the latter."

APPENDIX A: NOTES

— 1.2 —

fumble

Spadone says this about the three Fancies:
Fumble one with an other, on the
gambos of imagination between their legs.
(1.2.93-94)
Source of Above: Ford, John. *The Fancies, Chast and Noble*. Ed. Dominick J. Hart, New York and London: Garland Publishing, Inc., 1985.

Gordon Williams defines "fumble" as "grope sexually, coit with."

Source: Gordon Williams. *A Dictionary of Sexual Language and Imagery in Shakespearean and Stuart Literature: A-F*. London and Atlantic Highlands: The Athlone Press, 1994. Page 565.

<https://tinyurl.com/y5j3q76j>.

He explains in his entries on "fumble" and "fumbler" that the fumbling can be done incompetently or competently.

— 2.2 —

ringed mare

Spadone says this:

[Aside] 'Twould wind-breake a moyle,
or a ring'd mare, to vie burthens with her. (2.2.145-146)
Source: Ford, John. *The Fancies, Chast and Noble.* Ed. Dominick J. Hart, New York and London: Garland Publishing, Inc., 1985.
This is Dominick J. Hart's note on "ring'd mare":
A mare so fitted with metal rings as to prevent her from being bred.
Source of Above: Ford, John. *The Fancies, Chast and Noble.* Ed. Dominick J. Hart, New York and London: Garland Publishing, Inc., 1985. Page 226.

***

Here is a reference to "ringed mare" in a passage about paraphimosis, which occurs when a stallion is unable to retract its penis. Paraphimosis can occur:
[...] from vain attempts to cover a ringed mare (jumet bouclée) [...]
Source of Above: George Armatage, *Every Man His Own Horse Doctor*: London and New York: Frederick Warne & Co., 1894. Page 432.
<https://tinyurl.com/yybzvbdg>.
The same passage occurs earlier in this source:
William Percivall. *Hippopathology: a treatise on the disorders and lameness of the horse, Volume 2.* London: Longman Orme, Brown, Green, and Longmans, 1840. Page 383.
<https://tinyurl.com/y5wtyzc4>.

***

The *Oxford English Dictionary* defines one meaning of "ringed" in this way:
To attach rings to (a mare) so as to prevent her from being covered by a stallion. Obsolete.

— 3.1 —

Prugnioli ... Prugnuolo ... Pragnioli

Nitido says this:

"Seignior Prugnioli!" (3.1.64 or 3.1.65)

Source of Above: Ford, John. *The Fancies, Chast and Noble.* Ed. Dominick J. Hart, New York and London: Garland Publishing, Inc., 1985.

***

The Dyce/Gifford edition has "Signor Prugnuolo!"

It also has this note:

Here the 4to has "Prugnioli," and towards the conclusion of the play (p. 320) "Prugniolo's." Gifford printed "Pragnioli." (In Italian prugnuolo *means* a kind of mushroom*). D.*

Source of Above: *The Works of John Ford. Volume 2. Love's Sacrifice. Perkin Warbeck. The Fancies Chaste and Noble.* Edited by Alexander Dyce, William Gifford. Piccadilly: James Toovey, 1869. Page 267.

<https://tinyurl.com/yyuvdm9r>

***

One meaning of the Italian word *prugnolo* is "St. George's mushroom."

Source: <bab.la>. Accessed on 21 October 2019.

<https://en.bab.la/dictionary/italian-english/prugnolo>.

— 5.2 —

fumbling

Morosa says this to the three Fancies:

Young blood

Stand fumbling?

(5.2.62-63)

Source of Above: Ford, John. *The Fancies, Chast and Noble*. Ed. Dominick J. Hart, New York and London: Garland Publishing, Inc., 1985.

Gordon Williams defines "fumble" as "grope sexually, coit with."

Source: Gordon Williams. *A Dictionary of Sexual Language and Imagery in Shakespearean and Stuart Literature: A-F*. London and Atlantic Highlands: The Athlone Press, 1994. Page 565.

<https://tinyurl.com/y5j3q76j>.

He explains in his entries on "fumble" and "fumbler" that the fumbling can be done incompetently or competently.

APPENDIX B: ABOUT THE AUTHOR

It was a dark and stormy night. Suddenly a cry rang out, and on a hot summer night in 1954, Josephine, wife of Carl Bruce, gave birth to a boy — me. Unfortunately, this young married couple allowed Reuben Saturday, Josephine's brother, to name their first-born. Reuben, aka "The Joker," decided that Bruce was a nice name, so he decided to name me Bruce Bruce. I have gone by my middle name — David — ever since.

Being named Bruce David Bruce hasn't been all bad. Bank tellers remember me very quickly, so I don't often have to show an ID. It can be fun in charades, also. When I was a counselor as a teenager at Camp Echoing Hills in Warsaw, Ohio, a fellow counselor gave the signs for "sounds like" and "two words," then she pointed to a bruise on her leg twice. Bruise Bruise? Oh yeah, Bruce Bruce is the answer!

Uncle Reuben, by the way, gave me a haircut when I was in kindergarten. He cut my hair short and shaved a small bald spot on the back of my head. My mother wouldn't let me go to school until the bald spot grew out again.

Of all my brothers and sisters (six in all), I am the only transplant to Athens, Ohio. I was born in Newark, Ohio, and have lived all around Southeastern Ohio. However, I moved to Athens to go to Ohio University and have never left.

At Ohio U, I never could make up my mind whether to major in English or Philosophy, so I got a bachelor's degree with a double major in both areas, then I added a Master of Arts degree in English and a Master of Arts degree in Philosophy. Yes, I have my MAMA degree.

Currently, and for a long time to come (I eat fruits and veggies), I am spending my retirement writing books such as *Nadia Comaneci: Perfect 10*, *The Funniest People in Comedy*, *Homer's* Iliad: *A Retelling in Prose*, and *William Shakespeare's* Hamlet: *A Retelling in Prose*.

By the way, my sister Brenda Kennedy writes romances such as *A New Beginning* and *Shattered Dreams*.

APPENDIX C: SOME BOOKS BY DAVID BRUCE

Retellings of a Classic Work of Literature

Arden of Faversham: A Retelling

Ben Jonson's The Alchemist: *A Retelling*

Ben Jonson's The Arraignment, or Poetaster: *A Retelling*

Ben Jonson's Bartholomew Fair: *A Retelling*

Ben Jonson's The Case is Altered: *A Retelling*

Ben Jonson's Catiline's Conspiracy: *A Retelling*

Ben Jonson's The Devil is an Ass: *A Retelling*

Ben Jonson's Epicene: *A Retelling*

Ben Jonson's Every Man in His Humor: *A Retelling*

Ben Jonson's Every Man Out of His Humor: *A Retelling*

Ben Jonson's The Fountain of Self-Love, or Cynthia's Revels: *A Retelling*

Ben Jonson's The Magnetic Lady, or Humors Reconciled: *A Retelling*

Ben Jonson's The New Inn, or The Light Heart: *A Retelling*

Ben Jonson's Sejanus' Fall: *A Retelling*

Ben Jonson's The Staple of News: *A Retelling*

Ben Jonson's A Tale of a Tub: *A Retelling*

Ben Jonson's Volpone, or the Fox: *A Retelling*

Christopher Marlowe's Complete Plays: Retellings

Christopher Marlowe's Dido, Queen of Carthage: *A Retelling*

Christopher Marlowe's Doctor Faustus: *Retellings of the 1604 A-Text and of the 1616 B-Text*

Christopher Marlowe's Edward II: *A Retelling*

Christopher Marlowe's The Massacre at Paris: *A Retelling*

Christopher Marlowe's The Rich Jew of Malta: *A Retelling*

Christopher Marlowe's Tamburlaine, Parts 1 and 2: *Retellings*

Dante's Divine Comedy: *A Retelling in Prose*

Dante's Inferno: *A Retelling in Prose*

Dante's Purgatory: *A Retelling in Prose*

Dante's Paradise: *A Retelling in Prose*

The Famous Victories of Henry V: A Retelling

From the Iliad *to the* Odyssey: *A Retelling in Prose of Quintus of Smyrna's* Posthomerica

George Chapman, Ben Jonson, and John Marston's Eastward Ho! *A Retelling*

George Peele's The Arraignment of Paris: *A Retelling*

George Peele's The Battle of Alcazar: *A Retelling*

George's Peele's David and Bathsheba, and the Tragedy of Absalom: *A Retelling*

George Peele's Edward I: *A Retelling*

George Peele's The Old Wives' Tale: *A Retelling*

William Shakespeare's 38 Plays: Retellings in Prose

William Shakespeare's 1 Henry IV, aka Henry IV, Part 1: *A Retelling in Prose*

William Shakespeare's 2 Henry IV, aka Henry IV, Part 2: *A Retelling in Prose*

William Shakespeare's 1 Henry VI, aka Henry VI, Part 1: *A Retelling in Prose*

William Shakespeare's 2 Henry VI, aka Henry VI, Part 2: *A Retelling in Prose*

William Shakespeare's 3 Henry VI, aka Henry VI, Part 3: *A Retelling in Prose*

William Shakespeare's All's Well that Ends Well: *A Retelling in Prose*

William Shakespeare's Antony and Cleopatra: *A Retelling in Prose*

William Shakespeare's As You Like It: *A Retelling in Prose*

William Shakespeare's The Comedy of Errors: *A Retelling in Prose*

William Shakespeare's Coriolanus: *A Retelling in Prose*

William Shakespeare's Cymbeline: *A Retelling in Prose*

William Shakespeare's Hamlet: *A Retelling in Prose*

William Shakespeare's Henry V: *A Retelling in Prose*

William Shakespeare's Henry VIII: *A Retelling in Prose*

William Shakespeare's Julius Caesar: *A Retelling in Prose*

William Shakespeare's King John: *A Retelling in Prose*

William Shakespeare's King Lear: *A Retelling in Prose*

William Shakespeare's Love's Labor's Lost: *A Retelling in Prose*

William Shakespeare's Macbeth: *A Retelling in Prose*

William Shakespeare's Measure for Measure: *A Retelling in Prose*

William Shakespeare's The Merchant of Venice: *A Retelling in Prose*

William Shakespeare's The Merry Wives of Windsor: *A Retelling in Prose*

William Shakespeare's A Midsummer Night's Dream: *A Retelling in Prose*

William Shakespeare's Much Ado About Nothing: *A Retelling in Prose*

William Shakespeare's Othello: *A Retelling in Prose*

William Shakespeare's Pericles, Prince of Tyre: *A Retelling in Prose*

William Shakespeare's Richard II: *A Retelling in Prose*

William Shakespeare's Richard III: *A Retelling in Prose*

William Shakespeare's Romeo and Juliet: *A Retelling in Prose*

William Shakespeare's The Taming of the Shrew: *A Retelling in Prose*

William Shakespeare's The Tempest: *A Retelling in Prose*

William Shakespeare's Timon of Athens: *A Retelling in Prose*

William Shakespeare's Titus Andronicus: *A Retelling in Prose*

William Shakespeare's Troilus and Cressida: *A Retelling in Prose*

William Shakespeare's Twelfth Night: *A Retelling in Prose*

William Shakespeare's The Two Gentlemen of Verona: *A Retelling in Prose*

William Shakespeare's The Two Noble Kinsmen: *A Retelling in Prose*

William Shakespeare's The Winter's Tale: *A Retelling in Prose*